A CRY FOR

INDEPENDENCE

JOY K. MASSENBURGE

All rights reserved.
ISBN: 1985277883
ISBN-13: 978-1985277885
Copyright © 2018 Joy K. Massenburge

DEDICATION

Much love to my husband Elvin, my biggest
cheerleader, lover, and friend.

CONTENTS

CHAPTER ONE

"Surprise!"

Tammie Morris stumbled to a halt, body out of sync with her brain—a synapses misfire.

"Welcome home." Aunt Freda, Goodie Grandma, friends, and neighbors yelled in unison, talking over one another. All but one.

Tall as the door jamb behind him, Quan Blanton Sr., otherwise known as Q, held one side of the Welcome Home sign, eyeing her with his sultry gaze. A cocked brow accented brown eyes so bright they glowed. His bald head glistened, smooth milk chocolate.

Tammie blinked. Not even an hour after leaving the battered women's shelter, her heart lurched, then melted like it always did for her high school sweetheart. She cringed—what a pathetic start to the independence she'd mapped out for herself in an elaborate five-year-life-plan.

A brief shadow altered Q's initial appreciative look. Was it pity? Tammie lifted her chin to give him a full view of the permanent damage her face had sustained. At least she could see.

Q may not have been the one who had physically battered her, but his leaving her and Quan, Jr. nearly five years ago had crippled her far worse than the crushed eye socket and broken ribs she'd recently suffered at the hands of her ex-boyfriend, Fred Jeffers. Squaring her shoulders, Tammie glared at Q, momentarily forgetting their son held the sign's opposite end.

Confusion lined Quan, Jr.'s brow.

Had he witnessed the anger she'd directed at his father? She'd have to be more careful with her facial expressions around her son. Tammie gifted her son with the first real smile of the day.

Twelve months they'd lived apart, limited to visits worked in with school activities and her sister's schedule permitting her to make the three hour trip. Quan, Jr. had been over the male age limit to stay with her at the one shelter with any room. Not that she'd have been able to care for him properly.

Fred had almost killed her. Then there were the surgeries and recovery time. She rubbed a hand over her aching chest. If her sister and brother-in-law hadn't taken him in, where would Quan, Jr be?

Too soon, thick arms scooped her in close, trapping Tammie's face against a colossal bosom drenched in the familiar smells of home. Friday evening meal preparations of something beefy seasoned with bell peppers and garlic set her mouth to watering. "Tee, you didn't have to throw me a party. Just letting me live here until my place is ready is more than I can repay."

"That's what sisters are supposed to do."

Squirming free, Tammie spoke close to Tee's ear. "What's Q doing here? He's got six mo', *more*, months." She corrected herself, compliments of the employment preparation courses she'd taken at the center.

Tee made a big show of smooching Tammie loud on the cheek as she darted a glance around the room before whispering back. "Not now. A lot has happened in twelve months. Enjoy the party. Follow my lead. Your son is watching." Then she turned, opening her arms wide, and announced in a booming voice, most likely so everyone else could hear, "Welcome home, baby girl!"

Family, friends, and neighbors alike vied for kisses and hugs, but no Quan, Jr. She peered around heads and over big hairdos to find her son still standing on the chair holding his end of the welcome sign. Why didn't he come to greet her?

Greet and go. Tammie nodded, waved at others and kept walking toward her son. Quan, Jr. had grown, all arms and legs, like his father. She unconsciously touched the keloid scar raised beneath her eye and groaned. What mother wanted to be the source of their child's nightmares?

Uncle Joe tugged her arm. "What a treat for these old eyes."

Tammie jumped at his touch. She tried to cover her shock with a slight lift of her lips, but her jaw muscles cramped. Would she ever stop feeling the results of that horrific night? The results of a pitiful excuse for a relationship endured to keep a roof over her head and food on the table? Pretend came at a price. Maybe Fred had always known her heart belonged to another.

A tingle ran up and down her neck, her inner alarm someone watched her. She could turn around but it wasn't necessary. Only Q's gaze had ever infiltrated her body with heat, shudders, and butterflies so thoroughly. Instead, Tammie looked down at her hunched relative. "Thanks, Uncle Joe. It's good to be home, and back with my boy." She turned to go, but the thick–knuckled, withered hand held firm.

"I see Q done made it out. Y'all can be the family y'all should have been. Then that Fred would'na—"

"Excuse me." She knelt and caught her son as he finally ran into her arms.

Tears she'd rather save for later sprung from her eyes and dropped to Quan, Jr.'s smooth cheek. Relief flooded her heart.

He didn't hate her. The room appeared brighter, lifting her heavy spirit.

As if her uncle words called to him, Q crossed the room with a folded Welcome sign and handed it to Tee. Why was he here? His presence had her mind conjuring all kinds of scenarios. Would he try to poison Quan, Jr. against her? Time changed people.

She snuggled her son tight, inhaling the outdoor freshness that must've clung to his Dallas Cowboy's jersey from a recent romp in the backyard.

"I missed you." Tammie squeezed tighter. "So much."

He coughed. "Mom, I can't breathe."

A forgotten serenity trilled, filling her ears with the rare sound of her own laughter. "You shouldn't feel so good." She swiped away a tear with one hand. The other around her son, refusing to be separated from him.

He twisted loose but didn't try to make extra space between them. He looked her over.

Tammie startled when his hand drifted to her face, yet she kept her own hands at her sides. Tiny fingers explored the warped side of her eye with the lightest touch. They could have been the soft powder puff she'd used earlier to dust on the ebony minerals used to help conceal the distortion beneath.

"Does it hurt?" His innocence warbled.

A lump lodged in Tammie's throat.

"Let your mom get to her feet, son." Q stretched out his massive hand toward her.

Tammie took it, only after she began to see white spots. She couldn't drag enough air in past the lump in her throat to keep the room from tilting.

"Whoa!" He leaned toward her to anchor her unsteady stance.

Her head, clearing 5'8", rested on his sculpted pec' muscle. His manly spice settled in around her like a thick fog making her forget for a moment how he'd let her down when she'd needed him most. Tammie pushed hard against steel abs—prison life's physical tattoo—gasping for the air his proximity had stolen. "I can stand on my own."

He jerked back. "Tam, I just wanted to help."

Quieting her traitorous heart for its unwanted loyalty to Q, she lashed out with a deadly tongue. "For how long? Until your next relative needs you to take a drug charge?"

"My father—"

"Your son, Q. What about him?" She bit down, not willing to say another word. Q didn't owe her an explanation. Demanding one meant she cared. She didn't. The corners of her eyes stung.

A yank at the hem of her shirt stopped Tammie from making a fool of herself. She'd cried over Q for too many times. She turned and looked down into her son's wide-eyed gaze.

"Mom, aren't you glad the three of us gon' be a family, again?"

She gripped Quan, Jr.'s trembling shoulders and locked gazes. "Who told you that?"

***

Q fidgeted with what he should say. Now might not be a good time to declare his love for her or the plans he had for their future. The spiel he'd practiced—gone. A bumbling school boy he'd never been, but how else could he describe his discomfort?

Man up!

He cleared his throat and made sure to speak low. "Can we talk?" Q looked around the large living area. It covered most of the lower level which he had helped clear of furniture to set up tables and chairs.

From the corner, childish giggles erupted from the gossip trio, Shunta, Vette, and Latoya, friends from their high school days. Their laughter charged the room with friction. Q grimaced. He didn't have patience for their immaturity or the added drama.

"It's crowded in here. The kitchen, maybe?" His confidence wavered under this new icy disdain of hers.

"No." Tammie drew their son between them like a human shield.

Q's chest muscles tightened. The wary eyes before him belonged to a stranger. Did she really think he'd hurt her? So much had changed. She'd changed. His Tam had always trusted him, idolized…

He'd changed. No more living for Q and what others could do for him. This time, he'd serve and protect. Love her the way Christ loved the church. She'd been the giver and he the taker. Not this time around. But she didn't know that yet. If only she'd allow him another chance.

"Can I get you some punch?" Q stuffed his thumbs into the front pockets of his jeans and rocked on his heels.

"No, thank you." She tucked her dimpled chin and turned the left, scarred side of her face away from his view.

Thank God Fred Jeffers wasted behind bars. *Punk.* Q's thoughts wavered between his desire to forgive and images of snapping the guy's neck. It'd be best to put the guy out of his mind. One word to a member in his father's crew and the joker would be dead. But then someone would retaliate. He'd lived that life, but he wanted more for his son. His body ran hot. Q yanked at the collar of his blue polo shirt. He needed some air.

Help Lord! How would he ever convince Tammie he was a new man if he entertained his old ways of thinking? If only Q'd been there, Fred never would have entered his family's life. "If you need anything, let me know and I'll get it." Q backed away. "Until then, I'ma give you and Junior some room to get reacquainted."

He made his way to the food table and snagged a couple hot wings and Ranch dressing. Someone bumped his arm. Q turned to his right.

"You good, man?" Tee's husband, Deacon Spenser, or Deac as Q called him, held out a napkin. "Give her some time. Remember what we've been learning. Trust is earned. Tammie's been through a lot."

"You saw us just now?"

Deac piled beef sliders and chips on his plate. "Loosen up, it's a party."

"I'll try." Q searched the room for Tam and Junior.

The high school trio surrounded her and his son. At least, from what he could tell, Tam treated everyone the same—guarded, head tucked and face hidden.

"Join me upstairs for a game of bones." Deac nudged Q.

He dropped his head, giving up his vigilant watch over his family and faced his friend and mentor. "Old man, you ain't ready."

"See you at the table."

One last glance her way and Q ladled a cup of punch and followed Deac into the game room.

Clack! A heavyset brother cued a ball into the corner pocket of the pool table centered beneath a suspended six count billiards light fixture. Deac motioned to an unoccupied card table to the right of the room with a tin of dominoes. Q joined him and pulled out a chair, and sat opposite Deac.

Deac slammed a domino on the table. "Three times the lady, give me fifteen. You come to play or not?"

"She's changed." Q drew from the pile.

Deac saluted him, then slapped the table. "Christmas time, give me twenty-five."

Q shook his head and blew out a loud deflated breath.

"Retreat when challenged? If that's how you play the game, you'll never win your family back. Didn't you say God told you to marry Tam, or are you caught-up with her changed outer appearance?" Deac laid the ivory tiles face-down on the table and leaned back in the metal chair.

"I wasn't referring to her looks. She can't help what that wuss done to her." Q grunted and dumped his tiles. He rubbed the indented grooves in his palms from fisting the dotted ceramics too tight. "She's hard."

"Come on man. You get the girl pregnant her senior year in high school. Her family turns her out. Quan, Jr. was three when you got locked up. She worked two and three crappy jobs trying to keep that raggedy apartment you left her in. She has a reason to be hard."

Q slouched in his seat beneath a weight of regret at Deac's words. It was difficult to hear the role he'd played in destroying the gentle, selfless Tam he'd grown-up with.

Deac must have known the game was over when he two-armed the game pieces and raked them into a small pile. One-by-one, he refilled the tin storage container.

At the door, giggles and high-pitched voices infiltrated his sanctuary. Q stiffened and made a point not to look their way. Then a hand ran down his neck and manipulated the taunt muscle in his right shoulder.

Q spun around and locked gazes with Tam's accusing stare from the doorway as Vette leaned in too close.

"We wanted to know if you and Quan, Jr. plan to compete in this year's July Fourth basketball tournaments at the church. My son has his heart set on playing with you." She shared a knowing look with her posse.

Exactly what she knew, he had no clue, but her not so subtle invitation was not welcomed. "I haven't made any plans." Q shrugged Vette's hand from his shoulder.

She had the audacity to pout.

He stood to go after Tam.

Too late, she grabbed Junior's hand and fled the room.

Q turned back to the table. "Catch you later, Deac. Gotta go."

Downstairs, Q found people to greet so his conversations could lead to an indirect inquiry regarding Junior. If he found his son, the mother would be near. Everyone had more information than he'd asked for and nothing in regard to the information he'd requested.

Patience at a zero, Q approached Tee. "Have you seen Tam?"

"Kitchen." She carried a refilled chip platter toward the food table.

"Junior." Q called to his son upon entering the room.

Tammie jumped, steaming darkness sloshed from her cup onto the granite island. She unwound a fistful of paper towel to mop the spill.

What was the brown stuff? He'd never known her to drink coffee, or tea.

Tam frantically scrubbed the rock counter top and slumped onto the floor dabbing the moisture from the concrete scored floors. She probably needed the caffeine like some relied on nicotine or alcohol to cope.

Junior looked at Q. "Sir?"

"Go find your cousins and give me and your mom a chance to talk."

"Yessir." He hopped down from the barstool.

Q ran his hand over the boy's head as he passed, proud to see his likeness—a mirror image of himself. He had to get this right. For Junior. For Tammie. For himself. Q glanced into the ceiling.

Now's a good time to lead me. I'm at a loss here.

He crossed the room just as she dropped the soiled napkins into the waste basket and resettled into her chair at the bar as if she'd never been disturbed. Q took the seat his son had vacated next to her.

Tam sipped.

"Why did you run off?" Had he witnessed jealousy? Q fished for a sign that she still cared for him, but she masked her feelings well.

She swiveled her stool and faced him. "What on earth are you talkin' about?"

"You've never been one to play games, let's not start now." He reached to touch her cheek and checked himself.

A wall erected itself in her stiff, hiked shoulders. "Get used to it. A lot of things 'bout me ain't the same." She turned back to her cup and fingered the rim. "Make out with all the women you want. You're a free man. Me and Quan good. Don't need you. After tonight, if I never see you again, it'd be too soon." She drank.

"Sooner than later, then. Since I live here, I plan to do whatever it takes to change your mind."

Tam snapped her neck around and spewed warm liquid into Q's face and down the front of her shirt, coughing. "You live *where*?" She croaked.

Q licked his lips. Coffee. The brown liquid she drank had a name.

CHAPTER TWO

"Don't touch me." Tammie dodged Q's hand. He'd armed himself with paper towels, and she grabbed her own handful from the dispenser on the kitchen bar. How many spills would she clean up tonight? "Tend to yourself before you stain the rest of my clothes."

Coffee dripped from his long lashes. She'd gotten him good. Near tears again, rather than wipe her shirt front, she covered her flaming face with the abrasive paper.

If only it were embarrassment that made her treasonous body tingle. His nearness demanded a response. She had to live under the same roof with … his bass voice, rock abs, and vivid memories of loving this man?

"Tam, look at me." Q's consoling tone never failed to reach beyond her defenses.

She dropped her hands, clutching crumpled, make-up covered towels, and moved to face her son's father. "Why?"

"Because I want the truth." He caressed the side of Tammie's face. She snapped her head left, but she failed to shake his gentle touch loose. "Am I too late to fix things between us?"

He'd always been so sure of himself. When had he ever asked anything? The first day of her freshmen year at a new high school, he'd introduced himself and told her she'd be his girl. When she got pregnant, he'd told her they'd keep the baby and be a family. This new vulnerability confused her. Or maybe his closeness proved too distracting.

Tammie scrunched her eyes closed. *Hold me.* "Q, please. Don't."

Thank goodness his hand left her face and she released a tremulous breath. A moment more and she'd have been in his arms begging out loud for what her mind had just longed for. To help repair her mistakes. And what then… Wait for the day he'd let her down for a second time?

She opened her eyes, hoping to be more convincing. "I want to do things on my own. Independent of anyone's help. Just me and my boy." She pointed to the scars around her eye. "The last time I depended on someone to fix things it like-to-got me and my son killed."

He grabbed her hand. "Forgive me for not being there. I promise you I'm not the same foolish kid who left you to raise our son alone. I'm definitely not the monster that hurt you. Let me make things right. Junior needs me in his life."

Bile erupted in the back of her throat. "I get it now," she hissed, snatching her hand free. "How you convinced my sister to live here, I don't know. But the conniving ends today. You will not take Quan, Jr. from me!"

Q tried reaching for her hand, and she spun away.

Tammie pushed off the bar stool and stood over Q. "I'm not that naive kid who sat around all day waiting on you to pay my bills and make me feel like I was somebody." Her voice cracked. "Monday morning, I start my new job and will be able to support my son and me. I'm next on the list for an apartment. It should be ready soon. Just me and Quan, Jr. Your assistance is not needed. Not wanted!"

His arms snaked out around Tammie's waist before she could stop what was happening. Q stood, pulling her to his chest, caressing her back like he would a sullen child. She pressed against his torso with both hands to break free, but he didn't budge.

"Tam, stop." He leaned down close, cradling the fight out of her. "I'd never try to take Junior from you. I'm paroled here 'cause your sister helped set it up. I ain't running game on you, girl."

He pulled back and pinned her with a convincing stare. "Ask Tee. Her church has this program called Father's Heart where ex-cons like me learn stuff so Junior won't make the same mistakes. Wind-up where I did. Even helped me to get a good job at Brookshire's warehouse to support my family."

Through his shirt, she felt the thumping of his heart, racing to match hers. She couldn't sort out anything else, so close to him. She wrapped her arms around his back to brace herself, right? Then why, when his face brushed her cheek, did she turn and capture his bottom lip with hers? A sweet warmth engulfed her middle as he deepened the kiss.

Q moaned and pulled away. "I'm sorry. I shouldn't have."

Tammie shivered, immediately missing his warmth.

Why had he stopped? Did her scars repulse him? Confusion, then mortification washed over any remaining embers his closeness had sparked. Twelve months in the shelter, earning her GED with an independent life plan sketched out in her journal hadn't changed anything. She was still weak in behind Q. Vulnerable. Now he had proof.

She ran out the kitchen's back door.

"Tammie!" Q called.

***

The next morning, Q stuck his head through the door of Junior's room. "You about ready in here?"

"Yeah." Junior stood before the mirror, fumbling with the blue tie. They'd been practicing his tying technique.

"Yeah?" Q stepped in the room and moved to stand behind his son.

Junior smiled. "Yes, sir."

"Turn around." Q made the last loop, pulled the big end through, and pushed the tie's knot until it fit snug to Junior's little neck. "You almost had it. Soon you won't need my help." He ran a hand over Junior's close cut fade. "Where there's barely any hair on the sides, there's enough on the top to brush and make it wave."

"Yes, sir." He didn't waste any time but snagged a brush from his top drawer and raked it over his small head until the hair rippled.

Q sat on the twin bed. "I see you picked out your good suit. Ain't that a bit much for Children's Church?"

"I thought I'd get to go to big church with you and Mom."

What should he say? *Son, I messed up.*

After last night, Tammie wouldn't want to go anywhere with him. She'd run believing he'd take their son and probably thought he wanted to seduce her without the benefit of marriage. Q could have thumped his thick forehead with the palm of his hand—a V8 commercial in the making.

Last night, after she'd dashed away, he gave himself time to cool off. He'd waited until all the guests left before seeking her out, but turned from her bedroom door at the sound of muffled sobs. Q cracked his knuckles. Why his ardor challenged him when he held Tam, after it'd been non-existent for so long, he didn't even try to comprehend. Tam had always had that effect on him. He'd let his guard down. And let his son down in the process.

"Dad? Did you hear me?" Junior grunted.

Q shook his head. "Sorry. What did you say?"

"Do I get to go to church with y'all this time?"

"Your mom just got home and then there was the party last night. She'll probably sleep in. Why don't you change and save your suit for next Sunday? It's Family and Friends Day, anyway."

"Okay." As Junior yanked at his tie, Q slipped out of the room.

Regret dogged his heels all the way down the stairs, into the very kitchen where he'd lost his chance to be a testimony to his son's mother. The smell of bacon did nothing to lift his spirits as he slumped into his usual seat at the table for eight.

If he was honest with himself, he'd been looking for a reason to hold Tam close since she arrived at the party— tall, thick in the hips, and everything smooth dark mocha. Q stared at the empty bar stools. The passion he'd witnessed nestled deep in her gaze had been his undoing. Wanting to do things God's way and doing them were two entirely different things.

"Earth to Quan D'angelo Blanton Sr." Tee joined him at the table. "Someone looks like they need a cup of coffee. Did you get any sleep last night?"

"Did she tell you what happened?"

"What about some Vienna Roast first? Heavy cream and sugar, like you like it? Deac should be home from his momma's house with the baby by then."

"That bad, huh?"

"I was thinking of your comfort is all."

Q ran a hand over the stubble forming over his bald head. "Has Tam eaten?"

"Bright and early. She's probably with Quan, Jr. as we speak."

"I messed up." He buried his head in his hands.

Tee stroked his back. "You're being too hard on yourself." She left the table and returned with his mug.

Q rose and took the steaming cup from her hand and set it on the table. "Can you believe she thought I was scheming to take Junior from her?"

"I should have explained the situation to her, but the romantic idea of surprising her and it being a grand finale stole my good sense. We all learn from our mistakes." Tee returned to the stove and stirred something in a pot.

"Did you get a chance to talk to her last night?" Q twiddled his thumbs.

Tee removed the pot from the flames, then faced him. "Yes."

"One minute I was consoling her. The next, taking advantage of her." Q dropped his head.

"Really?" Tee's voice challenged. "I hear Tam kissed you, and you had to stop things before they got out of control. Correct me if I'm wrong."

Q stared at the groves in the oak table, imagining her tug his bottom lip as if it'd just happened. *Look Tee in the eyes, you ain't brand new.* "When I wrapped my arms around her, I knew what I was doing. Tam simply responded."

"Okay, there's shared attraction. Did you think that'd go away 'cause you got saved?"

"Well, yeah? How else can I witness to her?"

"The same way you buy groceries when you're hungry. You practice restraint until you make it home and prepare the meal."

"That's what I'm afraid of. The instant connection between us was an inferno before I had a thought to fight it. I don't know if I'll make it out of a next time."

"Get with Deac on some accountability check points."

The door from the garage into the kitchen opened. "Someone call my name?"

Tee rushed over to kiss the stout man on the cheek and scooped baby Devin into her arms. She covered the toddler's face with smooches until he squirmed to be put down.

"You act like the boy's been gone a week," Deac teased.

"Jealous?"

Deac crossed his arms. "Maybe."

Tee slid up next to her husband and planted playful kisses on his face.

"Save that for the boy. I'm a man." Deac grabbed Tee close, palmed the back of her head, and covered her mouth, showing his wife a man's kiss when Tam walked in, with Junior trailing.

"Yuck. Aunt Tee, you and Unc should take that to your room."

Tam slapped a hand over Junior's eyes. "Mind your business young man. Where did you learn such talk?"

Junior laughed.

Q waited in vain for Tam to look his way. Was she thinking of the kiss they'd shared last night? He was.

"Quan. Quan. Quan." Devin celebrated his cousin's name until Junior acknowledged his presence.

"Hey little man, give me five." Junior reached down and let the boy slap at his hand.

Q's chest inflated. His son would be a better man than him. He'd see to it. Correction, he'd see to it with God's help.

"Can I get another coffee this morning? Quan, Jr. insisted I join him for breakfast. My little man wouldn't take no for an answer." Tam spoke to her sister. "I wanted to discuss paying you some rent."

Tee dismissed her baby sister's proposal with the fling of her white drying towel. "Girl, stop talking foolishness and get you a cup."

Tam's light spirits encouraged Q to pursue Junior's earlier request. "What about you going to church with us this morning? We'd love to have you, wouldn't we, Son?"

She turned toward Q with fire in her eyes, and it definitely wasn't the passion of last night. "Can I speak to you in private?"

"Sure." Q darted a furtive glance at Deac who shrugged. Tee had already returned to her upscale professional stove. Had he spoken too fast?

Tam turned to Junior. "Give me a minute. What I need to say to your dad won't take long."

"Okay." Junior barely looked up from playing with his cousin.

Q followed Tammie out of the kitchen into the living area where the party tables had been removed. His leg bumped into one of the sectional, leather couches.

"How dare you try to make me look bad in front of my son, like you're the better? I hear you found religion in prison, but don't try to force it on me. You been out how long?" She flashed her splayed fingers in his face. "Five months? Let's see how long it lasts. You may have my sister thinking you changed, but I ain't so easily fooled."

"I deserve that. Especially after my behavior last night, you have every right to doubt I've changed. It won't happen again. But for Junior's sake, I thought you'd want to do things together. Give him the experience of a family."

"Like before? Look what that got him. A jailbird for a daddy."

Q clamped his teeth down hard. Needle sharp pain vibrated through his molars and pooled into the tender flesh of his gums.

Don't retaliate. "Keep your behavior excellent among the Gentile, so that in the thing in which they slander you as evildoers, they may because of your good deeds, as they observe them, glorify God in the day of visitation. 1Peter 2:12"

Q stomped away, the memorized scripture resounding in his head, and left her standing in the living area.

***

It won't happen again. Wasn't that what she wanted? *She* had kissed *him*. Dreamed of him. If he'd changed, then what did that make her? A shrew?

Tammie hugged herself and rocked back and forth, but it didn't settle the frustration boiling inside. Nice people finished last. She'd do well to remember that, but the hurt she glimpsed in Q's haggard features cracked her resolve.

Q was right, Quan, Jr. didn't need a hostile environment. He'd experienced enough of that with Fred.

Monday, she'd start her new job and be a step closer to getting her son the kind of life every kid deserved. She'd be the best employee, earn raises, and she and Quan, Jr. would be happy for the change—stability without any interruptions.

CHAPTER THREE

Tammie shifted in her seat. Would every morning be like this? No time for conversations. A quick kiss and goodbye to Quan, Jr. Then out the door and hustle to the bus stop several blocks from the house.

She huffed. Her cheeks, inflated like a puffer fish, released a stream of hot breath on her window of the stalled Tyler Transit. The moist ring lingered for a moment before fading. She lifted her arm and stole a quick peek. If her armpit rings dried as quickly as the window, that'd be good. She returned her gaze to the back of the bus driver's head.

"Hon, staring at that there bus driver ain't gone get this hunk of metal moving." The gray-haired lady reached past her granddaughter wedged between them on the front row seat and calmed Tammie's bouncing knee with a gentle pat. "That cloud of black smoke we saw is the big stuff. No quick fix."

Tammie grabbed the woman's vein-infused hand. "Do you by chance have a cell phone?"

"Matter of fact I do. Nothing fancy but it works in an emergency." She rummaged through her white handbag. "My children got it for me."

Tammie checked her watch. She didn't want to rush the nice lady but time was slipping away fast.

"It had to be the Christmas before last—"

"Can I please use your cell to let my job know I might be late?"

"Sure, hon."

She grabbed the flip phone and shook the lady's unsteady hand. "By the way, my name's Tammie Morris."

"Everybody calls me Mama Pearl." She released Tammie's hand.

"Thank you, Mama Pearl." Tammie turned back to the window, pulled the call center's business card from her purse, and dialed her supervisor.

The bus driver stood near the lifted hood, shaking his head, destroying Tammie's hopes of a miraculous repair and getting to work on time. "Yes ma'am, I'm going to be late. I'm really sorry. I'll get there as soon as possible." She snapped the phone closed.

"That didn't take long." Mama Pearl took her cell from Tammie and redeposited it into one of the many compartments of her bag. "They understood your dilemma, didn't they?"

"She said okay, but her tone gave me a different impression. It's my first day." Tammie stood. "Excuse me, I need to start walking."

"You'll sweat up a storm. That silky top you have on won't hide it well either."

"It'll have to do." Tammie smiled and pressed her way past the girl and her grandmother into the aisle. Out the doors and onto the curb, she squinted against the blast of sunshine.

Head down, she shuffled to the building they'd broke down in front of. Tammie pressed her back to the bricks shadowed beneath a green Unclaimed Furniture awning and paused, allowing her vision time to acclimate. A wave of vapors lifted from the concrete. Downtown Tyler could benefit from planting a few trees to block out the intense rays.

Standing in front of this store off Broadway, she didn't have too far to walk. But she'd be late. So much for making a good first impression.

Tammie looked at her feet stuffed into Tee's black heels that ran half an inch too short and grimaced. Until payday, she'd have to endure. The Nike Cross-trainers she owned didn't meet dress code.

She pushed off the wall and started walking. The sun beat on her bared skin making the back of her neck sting. She ignored it and trudged ahead until the light changed and the crosswalk displayed a "Don't walk."

A horn blared at the same time the walking man symbol turned white and signaled her to go. Tammie stumbled her first step as she ran across the red-bricked street. She stopped at the next curb, bent over at the waist, and rested her aching feet. A horn boomed again, but she couldn't move. Her pinky toes were on fire.

"Tam, get in. Let me give you a ride."

Q? She lifted to full height and turned to her left. It was him. Sitting in the driver's seat of a classic, maroon Monte Carlo, clean as if it were just driven off the lot.

Q called from the lowered passenger window and flaunted a brilliant smile.

Her breath caught. Like a damp stem of a firecracker, the retort she'd been ready to unleash fizzled out before she could voice it.

"Was that your bus that broke down back there?"

She flipped her left pump off and rubbed the offended appendage until it stopped aching. Then the right shoe before asking a question of her own. "Are you following me?"

Hooooonk!

Q leaned over and opened the passenger door. "I'm holding up traffic. Hop in."

"No, thank you."

"Get out the road! Some people have jobs to get to." A woman yelled from the sunroof of her car.

The old Q would have sprayed the lady with an arsenal of obscenities or even showcased his firearm, but this imposter apologized and motioned for the woman to go around.

Tammie's chest heaved with an extra burst of energy. "You heard her, get out the road. Some of us have a job to get to." His smile being contagious, Tammie lifted the corners of her mouth.

"You sure?"

"I told you once. Listen this time. I don't need any help. I got this." She waved him on much like he'd directed the angry commuter seconds earlier.

"All right." Q shut the door. "I know when I'm not wanted." He winked. "Let me know when I can be of service."

Q's words reeked with charm, and its pleading twang made her want to crawl into the car. "I won't." Tam hobbled ahead. Her head lifted high. She flipped her new bangs.

Like a shade-tree mechanic practicing the trade without a license, her cousin had come to the house last night and sewed in the hair extensions. It wouldn't do to frighten her co-workers on the first day.

When Q's car took the left turn ahead, she finally halted long enough to kick off the too little shoes, clutched them in one hand, and ran to the KLTV 7 Building, which housed the call center where she'd be starting her new job.

If she still had a job.

***

Q arrived a few minutes late to the Father's Heart morning session. He dragged himself into the vacant chair between Melvin Thompson and Ray Jones.

"Mr. Jones, have you been able to tell your son you love him?" Albert Anderson, the morning session mentor, jotted on his legal pad.

"I just don't see how that's healthy for a sixteen-year-old boy. He may start thinking it's okay to hug on other men."

Q slouched as his mind shut out Ray's words and flashed to the surprise party. He held Tammie tight against his chest. Her hair? It smelled sweet. Honey? Honeysuckle?

"Mr. Blanton, you're quiet. Is there anything you'd like to add to group today?"

Q bristled to attention. "Um. Let Catfish go and come back to me."

"Are you referring to Mr. Turner?" Mr. Anderson didn't need to raise his voice for Q to understand he'd been chastised.

"Sorry, I slipped up."

"Remember, you're not *Brughs* hanging on the streets anymore. Maturity has a look. A sound. Can you sit up straight and address your brothers formally as a respected peer for us *Mr. Blanton*?"

Q sat up taller in his metal, fold-out chair and recited the proper opener. "Mr. Anderson, I thank you for this opportunity to share. Brothers in Christ, greetings."

The group of five men gathered in the circle chorused. "We love you, and there's nothing you can do about it."

Sharp pin pricks rained over Q's skin whenever they had to recite the monthly quote. How could these men love him? Unlike the five-year-sentence he'd served protecting his rotten father, he'd done nothing to earn this love. Worse, why did he want their love and respect so much?

Q shook off his musings with a rippled crack of his knuckles. "I'm requesting prayer. My son's mother is back in my life, and I'm struggling to be the man God depicts in the Bible."

"Ah, come now, Mr. Blanton, you know we don't work in generalities here. Name your struggles. Others can learn from your testimony. This is not the time to be shy." Mr. Anderson spoke things in such an easy manner any man would feel pressured to cooperate.

"You got that right. Remember, Mr. Anderson say 'it's good for men to be vulnerable sometimes.'" Mr. Thompson high-fived Mr. Jones, blocking Q's view.

A roar of good-natured laughter rent the room. "Sounds like the kind of problem the church would make you marry your son's mother to solve." Mr. Turner elbowed Mr. Jones. "They say God understands your heart."

Mr. Anderson cleared his throat loudly, and the room quieted. "Careful, gentlemen. This is a safe place to discuss our struggles, right?"

Heads around the building nodded.

"That's just it. I want Tam to see I've changed." Q bent over, letting his head hang low for a few seconds before raising to face the accountability of the brethren.

"What's stopping her from seeing?" Mr. Anderson prompted.

"Me." He ran a hand over his freshly shaven head. "Images of her body, the way she feels, smells… Grrrrr!" Q clenched his fists. "The torment. It's both mental and physical. How do I witness when I'm so weak? There's nothing godly going on in my mind."

The room quieted around him as if the others present shared in his anguish. One by one, heads bowed. Some lips moved. He'd tried to pray since leaving Tam on the street corner an hour ago. The words wouldn't form. Q slammed his eyelids shut. Hopelessness punched him in the gut.

Had he really changed? How long before he'd be back on the streets, doing the biddings of his dope dealer father?

Mumbled pleas to God pulsed around him. And didn't stop for some time. The cadence of their one accord silenced the mental rantings of self-doubt as his brothers shouldered his burdens. Q rolled his head forward, to the side, back, and around. The strain he'd carried into the church's Annex Building finally fled.

Thank you, Lord. Your grace sustains, right?

Q, too tired to speak, opened his eyes, exhaled, and rested in the presence of friends. This must of have been what Proverbs meant by the Lord being a strong tower and the righteous running into it and being safe.

***

Tammie lugged her shoeless dead dogs into the house through the kitchen entrance off the garage. She would've flung the battered pumps dangling from her pointer finger across the room, if Tee hadn't been enthroned in front of the stove.

Instead, she stopped, closed her eyes and sucked a delightful aroma through her nostrils. Cinnamon. Butter. Tons of it. With each inhale, she gained a pound.

Rounded hips swinging and Tee humming an upbeat tune, she stirred the concoction. "I wish you'd let me pick you up after work. The bus route traffic and frequent stops add over an hour to your work day. Junior won't have long to spend with you before its time for him to go to sleep."

"And how was your day?" Tammie didn't succeed in keeping the edge from her words. The sharpness set her ears to ringing.

Tee's hand stilled, along with the happy hips and joyous hums. She whirled around. Her face pinched. "You're right. I'm sorry. How was your day?"

"Don't ask." Tammie burst out laughing. Tee frowned, and Tammie laughed harder. Maybe she had lost her mind, just a little. To keep from crying, she might as well.

Tee dropped her spatula on the stove top. She cleared the distance between them to hover her concerned gaze upon Tammie. "Are you having a nervous breakdown?"

"Not that I know of. Maybe a little overwhelmed, but I think that's normal at this stage in my life." Tammie fell into her sister's chest when she stretched out her arms. For a moment, she let Tee shoulder the enormous burden she'd carried around all day like a cast iron ball chained to her ankle. "Anything that could go wrong, did."

"And here I go bombarding you the moment you enter the door. I let the devil use me." Tee rubbed Tam's back. "We'll work things out."

She pulled from Tee's embrace. "I've got to learn to do things on my own. When my apartment is ready, it'll just be me and Quan, Jr. I might as well learn how to do it now. I can't depend on people for the rest of my life."

"Everybody needs somebody along the way. My church members supported Deac and me with prayers and a listening ear throughout our fertility struggles. My in-laws have assisted me with Devin's care. When Deac got laid off a couple years back, his brother helped us financially."

Tammie held her hands up and shook her head. "Along the way is one thing. My entire life, I've depended on others. The cycle has to stop if things are going to change."

"Refusing help from your family or keeping Q out of your and Junior's life is not the answer. Your change will come when you relinquish control to Christ."

"Is that what Q told you? I've said no such thing."

"No, but if you're doing everything on your own, where does that leave the rest of us. Have you stopped to consider what Quan, Jr. needs?"

"Everything I do is for him."

"Is that so? Then why didn't you join him at church Sunday?"

"That was Q trying to make me look bad in front of my boy."

"Really? Well let's just see about that. Quan, Jr." Tee's voice boomed. When he didn't come, she bellowed again. "Junior, come here."

He rushed into the kitchen still dressed in his school uniform, white polo shirt paired with navy khakis. "Ma'am?"

Tee marched to stand in front of him. "When your dad asked your mother to go to church yesterday, whose idea was it?"

Quan, Jr.'s face lit up and a big toothy smile split his face. "Mine." Then he frowned. "But Dad told me to save my suit for next Sunday. He said Mom would be sleepy after the party." As if he had just realized her presence, Quan, Jr. turned a new smile on Tam. "Mom!"

She crossed the room on renewed feet as her son ran into her arms. "Hey, baby. Did you have a good day at school?"

"Yes, ma'am. But you weren't here when I got home. Where were you?" Disappointment pitched high in his voice.

Tammie couldn't hold his downtrodden gaze so she spoke to the tiled floor. "Work." She had nothing to be ashamed of. She'd worked two jobs when they lived with Fred. Then why did her answer sound pathetic in her own ears?

She looked up, as Tee watched her. How could she ever give her son the life he'd come to expect after living with her Susie Homemaker sister and Superman brother-in-law?

CHAPTER FOUR

If yesterday brought the blues, then she'd call today Terrible Tuesday. Tammie flocked next to a grandpa, two girls in waitress garb, and a smorgasbord of other working class employees stuffed beneath the bus stop overhang. Though rain soaked the streets, at least she had shelter.

Tammie covered her nose. Damp fibers infused with mix-matched fragrances and traces of breakfast clung to warm, cloistered bodies.

She stretched her neck to make the farthest end of the street visible. No Tyler Transit. Tammie nudged the man next to her. "It's a bit crowded. How long have you been waiting?"

"The six o'clock never showed." He pointed to a lady with a pink umbrella hanging from her wrist. "She called the office right before you came, and they said another should be here within thirty minutes."

Her chest tightened. Oh, no. Not only were they behind schedule, but with this many people some would be forced to wait for the next pick-up. Tammie stumbled forward as more commuters arrived and pushed their way to take cover.

Tammie stared at the woman's pink rain gear and berated herself. She'd seen the dark clouds. Her bottom lip stung, but she welcomed the pain and bit into the flaked skin until the familiar iron taste seeped into her mouth. If she walked back to the house in this storm, changed clothes, and asked Tee for a ride, she'd be late.

That's what you get for being so stupid.

Her supervisor wasn't going to accept transportation trouble again. Tammie let her head fall backward and grunted when it banged against the shelter's glass panel. Jerking her hand to rub the sting from her injured noggin, she hit the child next to her. "Sweetie, I'm *sooooo* sorry."

A hand pushed Tammie's out the way before she could help the little girl straighten her glasses. "You're sorry all right. Keep your hands to yourself." An older version of the girl screwed her nose up and yanked the kid to stand behind her.

Out of Tammie's reach.

Would that always be the story of her life? Post a sign on her back—Children Beware. Visions of Quan, Jr.'s battered body resurfaced. She closed her eyes, took what should have been a cleansing breath, and gagged. The tangy tide of sweet sulfur had morphed within the cramped space into the worst stink bomb she'd ever smelled. Eyes forced opened, Tammie slapped a hand over her mouth, barely holding onto Tee's heavy breakfast of pancakes and eggs.

"You don't look so good." The nice man she'd spoken to earlier put a supportive hand under her elbow.

"Nothing fresh air won't cure." *If only it could save my job.* Another thing out of her reach.

"Yeah, it's plenty stuffy and rank under here."

"I just wish I could get to work on time." Tammie spied Q's Monte Carlo. The window lowered.

"Tam!"

Rain poured into Q's car. Why didn't he raise the window?

"Tam!"

"Do you know the man in that car, young lady?"

Her heart did. It raced. Her middle, it melted. Who was she kidding? She still loved Q. And wanted the happily-ever-after he promised.

Wasn't that the problem? Giving in to feelings had left her a single mother. Then she'd let that monster, Fred, move into her home. Tammie couldn't trust her judgement. If choosing her desires led to failure, denying them should lead to the success she needed to turn her horrible life around.

The window raised. Then the driver's door opened. "Yes," she stammered. "I mean, yes, sir. I know him."

Q stepped out, popped open the massive umbrella, and strode toward the bus terminal. "Tam, come on. I'm giving you a ride to work."

She shook her head.

"I'm not going anywhere until you leave with me." Q beckoned with his hand. "Let's get you out of this storm. By the looks of things, you'll be late if you wait for that bus."

Again, she shook her head.

The gentleman that had been at Tammie's side since her arrival tapped her elbow. "I believe God heard your wish."

A chill ran down her spine. God didn't work in wishes, genies did. But she didn't believe in them either. None of that changed the fact Q stood before her offering a ride. The answer to her dilemma.

She took a step forward, separating herself from the crowd, and looked back. The nice man smiled.

Q must've taken that step to mean yes. He rushed to her side and draped an arm over her shoulder. Maybe she should've pulled away. Refused him. Nope, wasn't happening. Who could think with him so near?

Lost in Q's brown gaze as she was, the rain seemed to cease. She'd have sworn the sun broke free of the dark clouds as her body temperature raised. Shielded from the downpour, Tammie wrapped an arm around Q's trim waist and let him lead her to the passenger seat.

With tall confidence on sure feet, Q rounded the front of the car and took a seat behind the steering wheel. Nostalgia for the security and happiness they'd once shared took Tammie's breath and she coughed.

How had he known to come? They hadn't discussed her work schedule or bus route. She'd have to be in the same room with him to do so, and she had made sure that didn't happen. For this very reason—he got close and she caved.

Tee! She'd have to straighten out her sister when she got home. Tammie tried to clear her throat and started coughing anew.

Q's long arm stretched behind her seat. "Here. You need some water for that cough."

"Thank you." Tammie took the room temperature bottle from his grasp.

He pulled away from the curb.

Tammie flipped her bangs. "Do you even know where I work?"

"KLTV 7 Building downtown." His deep voice stroked away the last of her morning's anxiety.

Like a contented cat, she burrowed into her seat. Only thing missing was the purr. Since he knew everything, Tammie sat back and swigged her water.

***

Q checked his mirrors and changed lanes. Tam smelled so good. Reminded him of his favorite Passion Fruit bubble gum. *Focus.* "A little conversation would be nice."

She took a long draw from her water bottle. "What'cha wanna talk about?" She dropped the proper talk and spoke like the Tam he remembered.

Everything. Us. "Good morning to you, too. Missed you at breakfast."

"I like to get to the bus stop early." She wiggled under her safety belt.

"So, you're not avoiding me."

Tam looked out the window and bounced her knee.

Q tightened his grip on the wheel to keep from reaching over and grabbing her leg. If only she'd let him comfort her. "I can give you a ride to work every morning. At least to the corner across the street. I have to go that way anyway."

"Where to?"

He wouldn't force her to answer his first question. Anything to keep her talking. "I attend a men's accountability group at Tee's church. Remember? I told you about it."

"Father's Son or Fathers and sons." Tam shifted in the seat and faced forward. Her skirt hiked, displaying smooth, shiny skin.

Did she still oil down with baby oil gel after her shower?

"Q! Car."

He slammed the brake, and stretched a protective arm across the front of Tam. "Great eye."

"Where was your head just now? Obviously not on the road." She flipped her perpetually sagging bangs.

"Got distracted. I'm good now." Q rubbed the back of his neck. "You almost had it. The group is called

Father's Heart. I attend the morning sessions since I work from twelve noon until the job is finished. You and Junior have usually retired for the night when I come in."

"When do you sleep?"

She does care. He smiled so big, his teeth began to dry. "It's a rotating shift so I get two, four, or six days off to match the days I'm scheduled. Work hard and catch up on sleep later."

"Do you go to these meetings when you're off?"

"I—" If he told her he went to the afternoon meetings when he was scheduled off, she'd refuse his offer to take her to work on those mornings. How did he answer without lying? "I still go."

"Oh."

"On my days off, I'd like to pick you up. Before you say no, hear me out." Q braked for the red light. "I already get Junior from school. There's a coffee shop a couple blocks down where we can do homework and then scoop you up at five." The light turned green and he followed the traffic. "Maybe stop at the park on the way home and enjoy flying a kite in this windy weather."

She winced.

"What?" Q hit his brakes but didn't see any infractions he'd committed.

"I bit my bottom lip in the same spot I bit it earlier." She hated the nervous habit. A horrible reminder of her days with Fred.

"Explains the blood smattered on your lip. There's tissue in the glove box."

Tam retrieved the plastic packet and tugged the visor down. "Ummm. I'm not sure if we're ready for kite outings." She dabbed her lip.

He slowed for the red tail lights ahead—leaving plenty of space. "Think of Quan, Jr. He needs family time, even if you're not willing to factor me into your life equation."

Tam gripped the armrest between them as if they were on a free-falling roller coaster.

His throat ached. The struggle playing over her pinched features gained his compassion. He covered her hand. "We're in this together. I'm scared, too. I can't guarantee I'll never disappoint you. But Junior's worth the risk, don't you think?"

Tam again looked out the passenger window, but she didn't pull away.

Instead of bringing her smaller hand to his mouth the way he longed to, Q squeezed her fingers. And she held on. His face lifted into what he knew to be a big toothy grin. Such overwhelming hope couldn't be contained on the inside. It had to be shared.

Q freed her hand and parallel parked the Monte Carlo. He had to be quick, but made it to her side of the car just as she opened the door. "You're here with twenty minutes to spare." He extended a helping hand.

Tam accepted his help and stepped out. Her leg brushed his pant leg.

He didn't look down. He made the infamous bangs she now used to cover her face a focal point. "Since you'll be asleep when I get in tonight, I expect to see you at breakfast and then drive you to work."

"It shouldn't be raining tomorrow."

CHAPTER FIVE

Tammie peeked out her upstairs bedroom window into the backyard. Quan, Jr. wiggled his legs in an original victory dance inside the homemade end zone marked off with orange cones. Q rushed her son and hefted him into a tight bear hug. Quan, Jr.'s laughter palpitated along the glass. She pressed a hand to her sternum to no avail. The ache continued to spread.

"What happened to your migraine?" Tee startled Tammie from her hiding place behind the curtains into the opening in front of the window.

"My head did hurt, but I'm better now." She crossed the room and reached for her t-shirts piled on the bed and put them in her top drawer. Hopefully, no one playing outside saw her.

Tee took a few steps into the room and closed the door. "Uh-huh. Girl, go join your son or are you avoiding the tall, handsome, bald guy downstairs? It's Saturday.

Except for Deac, everyone is home. You can't hide all day."

"I hadn't planned to."

"Then why you folding clothes in here? Over the last four weeks you've done the task on the big table in the laundry room." Tee pointed to the bed. "Now you have a basket and hangers here in your room on standby. Only difference I see is Q being home. Stop me if I'm wrong."

How could she explain the tug and pull going on in her head? First, she'd given in to Q driving her to work. Now, he joined her for breakfast and she laughed and talked with him. Even played the happy family on his off days hanging out at the park with Quan, Jr.

What would happen when she moved? Would Junior, choose to remain with his dad? Would she be alone? She shivered.

Without a task to keep her hands busy, Tammie admired the ceiling's crown molding. The 42-inch flat screen mounted above the ornate chest of drawers had been silent all day. Maybe she'd ball up and sulk to a good sappy Hallmark movie like her mom had done when she was in her feelings.

"I don't get it. For weeks you've hung out with family like old times and now we're back to hide and seek.

Tell me what's stewing in that mind of yours before I start believing I'm crazy." Fisting her hips, Tee made her eyeballs cross until they tangled.

Tammie covered her face with one hand and squealed. "You know I can't stand it when you do that. Your eyes gon' get stuck in your head."

Tee laughed. "Then set them free." She sighed. "Tell me the truth. What's going on?"

Returning to the place just behind the curtain, Tammie spied Quan, Jr. at the drink cooler. A highlighter-yellow liquid funneled into his small plastic cup. She suspected it might be Gatorade.

"Is Q a better parent than me?"

"You're both good parents. See! This is what I mean. You're emotionally all over the place. Q is being Q. Has he said something to make you so skittish around him?" Tee joined Tammie where she stood looking out the window and stroked her arm. "If I'd known having Q paroled here would make you so uncomfortable, I wouldn't have asked him to come."

Tammie placed her hand over Tee's. "You did the right thing. Quan, Jr. is happy. Watch how he runs up to his daddy and waits for him to palm his head. And that smile. It's real." She wrapped her arms around herself and squeezed. "My boy didn't smile when I lived with Fred. More like a permanent grimace. I should have known what Fred was doing. I missed every sign."

"How could you know? You'd never been abused. You'd never seen our father raise a hand to Mother. You're not being fair to yourself."

"A *good* mother... knows." No matter how much she tightened her arms, regret spilled over her cheeks.

Tee tugged her arm.

Tammie fell into her sister's ready embrace.

"There, there. You're carrying a burden too heavy for you alone. Forgive yourself." Tee stroked her back. "God is waiting to take the load. Give it to him, sweet girl."

Although she didn't deserve her sister's assurances, the heaviness lifted from her chest. With tears spent and sniffles trailing behind, Tammie lifted her head and left the comfort of Tee's soggy shoulder.

Tammie plopped down in the center of the bed, making the box springs whine in protest. "How can it be? Quan, Jr. acts so normal. Watching him just now." She took a deep breath. "That kid's not big enough to have taken blows from a grown man." She lowered her voice. "Sorry, Tee, I just get so angry. We're working on it in my private counseling sessions at the aftercare center."

"I understand. But have you noticed? You're having fewer and fewer outbursts." With a twinkle in her eyes, Tee tucked her hands in the pockets of a flour dusted apron and walked to the head of the bed. "I've been tempted to ask why you're smiling when you come in from work. During your bus riding days, a haggard, foot-tired old lady limped in here."

The tips of Tammie's mouth lifted in spite of the gloom she'd allowed into her mood. "Don't start."

"Admit it. Q's a fresh breath of air. Changed. New."

"Almost too changed. Something about him makes me uncomfortable."

"Does it have anything to do with your renewed feelings for him?"

Best she steer this conversation in another direction. "My boy can't afford to get the wrong idea. Got a call, today. I'll be in my own place in a month. This whole set-up has made him think we're back together. And that can't be good for him."

"Y'all's living arrangements had nothing to do with Junior's so-called ideas. Your entire countenance lights up whenever Q enters the room."

"It does not." Tammie buried her face in her hands. Too often lately, Q had surprised her with a thoughtful word or funny joke that left her gasping for her next breath. "Beyond any feelings I may or may not have, I'm never totally comfortable around him. Like I need to watch my every word."

"It's the Holy Spirit. I remember a time I walked into a room and people stopped cussing and started apologizing to me. Complete strangers. I hadn't posted a sign, I'M A CHRISTIAN. They sensed God's presence in my life." Tee touched Tammie's chin and lifted. "I pray for the day that you will seek Him for yourself. The world's independence you keep harping about is a lie."

Tammie stared Tee down. "You're talking crazy. God has nothing to do with how I feel around Q or me becoming self-sufficient. Spirits? I've never even mentioned ghosts."

Tee ignored her sister's crack about ghosts. "Give me one example of how Q has changed, and I will show you the Holy Spirit's influence in his life."

Tammie stomped her feet like a cantankerous child. "Okay! Okay. When he looks at me but walks away." She stared at her fire-red toenails. Of all the things she could have shared. Maybe his rejection had bothered her more than she'd understood.

She'd trusted *that* look. Given her heart. Her body. And, yes. She craved to have that connection again with Q. It was the closest thing to peace she'd ever experienced. Even if only for a moment. "Never mind."

"Out with it, girl."

Tammie looked up, but couldn't voice her feelings. Let Tee save her judgements for the murderers and crooks. The bad people. She was one of the good ones. "He's changed."

Tee bent over and hooted.

"I don't see anything funny."

"Oh, Tammie, don't get all crabby. Let me explain what I mean." She huffed as if laughing so hard tired her out. "You're used to the old Q. He would've had you in this room and satisfied that itch. You both got it bad." Tee locked gazes. "I see what you think I don't."

Tammie studied her hands folded in her lap.

"The new and restored Q is showing you the respect due to a lady as God intended." Tee tapped her under the chin, and Tammie lifted her head. "Not because you're not desirable, but Q is learning to love the right way."

"I wasn't itching when I slept with Q. I loved him. He loved me. That's what people in love do."

"True love doesn't sample the produce before purchase. It honors the Word of God with marriage first. It commits." Tee fingered the bangs from over Tammie's eye. "He's not a slave to his desires anymore. The Holy Spirit, God living on the inside, helps Q to refrain. God fights his battles for him. Now that's liberty."

"For me, liberty is not being disappointed. Can your liberty keep him from walking out on me and Quan, Jr. again? Or was his leaving God's punishment for me getting pregnant?" Tammie hiked her chin high. "If that's the case, so be it. I love my son and don't regret his being born. If I'm a slave to anything, it's loving Q." She grabbed the edge of the mattress and fisted the comforter. "Even when Daddy kicked me out the house, nothing mattered as long as I had Q."

"Daddy was wrong, Tammie. On his death bed, he voiced his regrets. God changed his heart in the end, like God changed Q. I wish you would have gone to see him at the hospital. He wasn't the perfect parent, but he loved you."

Her throat closed. "That was a long time ago." Tammie's voice squeaked much like a scared mouse trapped in a corner. Take a hammer to her heart, and it would've crumbled.

How dare Tee mention that man? Her father…changed? Nobody changed that much. If she accepted her sister's theory, then she'd have to admit her own life was wrong. But she wasn't, was she? And she'd prove it. Starting with Q.

She'd been holding back, but no more. By the time the sun went down, she'd have Q in her bed, evidence God didn't live in him. Why itch when there was someone to scratch it?

"Tammie?"

"I need some time to myself. Ain't it close to Devon's nap time, anyway? Go. Go tend to baby." She hated the sorrow that dimmed her sister's eyes but she'd start screaming and throwing things if she had to endure her presence a second more.

"I didn't mean to hurt you." Tee worried the pocket on her apron, and walked out the door.

***

"Junior don't track dirt through the house. Stop by the laundry room and strip down to your undies, then go shower for dinner." Q collected the orange end zone markers. "Make sure you put 'em in our basket."

"Yes, Sir." He scrambled through the back door into the house.

Cones stacked and tucked beneath his arm, Q lifted his face and closed his eyes. The sun's rays heated his face. His prison days never far from his memories, he gave silent praise. *Thank you, Lord.*

Q stored their toys away in the garage and made his way into the laundry room. The house was quiet. Deac's truck gone. Tee probably napping with Devon. Where was Tam?

He separated their clothes into piles. Rather than hang out in the window, Tam should have come outside and spent some time with her son. Q sent a pair of Junior's jeans flying into the mound of black socks.

Towels, he threw into the master basket Tee had designated so she could launder them personally. *"Nobody washes my towels."* He chuckled. Less for him to do.

"Somebody's in a great mood."

Q turned at the sound of Tam's voice.

She seemed to float through the door, carrying an empty basket.

The base of his neck thumped. He couldn't hinge his jaw shut. Where was she going dressed so sexy?

Spring flowers bordered her white sundress. She had oiled her long arms, and legs. But her plump lips glistened like ripe grapes on display in the market, ready to be plucked.

"Q?" Whispery smooth and seductive, his name flowed from her plump lips.

"I am. In a great mood, I mean." His mind and mouth struggled to work together. "Howww are you?"

"Good." Tam twirled to the left, and racked her basket in its assigned spot on the wall, bringing temptation within touching distance. Up close, Tam's smile slipped and her eyes shone with frozen tears.

"No, you're not good." Q dropped the clothes from his hands and stepped to her side. "Talk to me."

Tam scrunched her nose.

Q sniffed the air. "Sorry." He stepped back and tucked his elbows into his sides. "Junior and I worked-up quite a stench. But you watched from the window, so why am I telling you something you already know?"

It took a moment, but the corners of her mouth lifted. This time soft and natural.

"That's my girl. See, life's not so bad."

"Am I?" Tam closed the distance and searched his gaze.

"Am I what?" Q's palms tingled. Did he answer? How did he make her understand the new relationship he wanted with her?

Q stepped back.

She advanced.

He exchanged steps with her until his legs bumped into the island. "Tam, what's wrong?"

"Am I still your girl?" She rested her head against his heart.

Yes. Q shut his eyes. Imprisoned by her words, he relived their forbidden passion. Everywhere her body pressed against his, he burned. "Tell me what's happened." He pleaded in a last attempt to redirect the destructive path he had no power to stop.

Tam ran her hands over his shirt front and around his back. "Nothing. I just want to be with you." She raised on her toes, and he met her lips.

Her mouth tasted like the nectar of the honeysuckles lining his grandma's back yard, but sweeter. She filled his arms but that wasn't enough. Blood coursed through his veins, rattling his eardrums. Q slid his hands along her curves, gathering her firmly against his chest and lifted, sitting her on top of the table.

Having raised his arms, a gust of musty onions snatched his next breath. Q stumbled back. What in the world?

"What's wrong?" Tam's swollen lips tempted him to rationalize his behavior.

He clutched the sides of his head and shook. "I messed up." He turned and splayed his hands on the wall. "Here I say I love you and I handled you worse than Fred ever did." He banged his forehead.

"Q stop."

"God, I'm a worthless cause." He flipped around, slid to the floor, and rested his head on his knees.

Tam knelt beside him and hovered over his lowered head. "It's okay. We didn't do anything."

"Don't waste your time on me. I really thought I'd changed." Q pressed his knuckles into the ceramic floor. "I was a bar of soap away from breaking my vow to God. How many times will I hurt the ones I love?" He avoided her eyes. Knowing he'd failed and seeing it reflected from her gaze would be more than he could take.

"Quan. D'angelo. Blanton. Senior."

He stilled. Chills ran down his back. She never used his full name.

Tears washed her face. Tam swiped her face, dried her hands on her dress, then extended one to him. "Tee was right. You're no longer a slave to your desires. She said your God lives inside you helping you to refrain from settling your itch until you're married. Your God *is* real."

Q choked and fumbled the offered hand. On the second attempt, he gripped and she pulled. On his feet, he tried to speak when she pressed a finger over his mouth.

"How do I get Him to be my God?"

"What?" Q couldn't remember what he'd said to get here. She asked a question but her finger still ramrodded his mouth shut. This day had slipped away from him. Maybe *he* needed a nap. Then, he could think straight.

"Just tell me how you got God," she insisted.

Q moved her finger from his lips and wiped his face. He struggled to breathe. The air in the room—so charged with passion—it did nothing to clear his fuddled mind.

"I'm sorry." She turned and paced the room.

He managed two full breaths. "I need to apologize to you." He worked to get his words in the conversation.

"First, tell me one thing." She pulled her bangs back. "Did my scar repulse you just now?"

"No. I forget it's beneath there. Your scar has no bearing on my feelings for you."

"Tee was right."

He ran a hand over his head. "I'm confused."

"Me, too. You've been trying to get me to attend church, but can't tell me how you got God. I don't get it."

Q walked over to the island and sat on the countertop. Breathe."It was while I was in prison." He toyed with a bottle of stain remover. "A visiting preacher had come. He told me God wanted to change my heart. All I had to do was surrender my will."

"How do you do that?"

"I said the sinner's prayer asking God to forgive me and come into my heart. Give me love for my hate." He pounded his chest. "Be my God." Emotion throbbed through him. "Instead of pledging myself to my father's gang family, I gave my loyalty to Him." He pointed to the ceiling. "I'm sure our relationship started there. But I didn't believe it until I was able to forgive my father. Since he wouldn't visit, I sent a letter."

She slapped her hand over his mouth. "Forget I asked." Had he heard her conversation with Tee earlier? "I'll barf if I hear one more dead, father forgiveness story. And please, get in somebody's shower." Tam stomped out.

CHAPTER SIX

Tammie shut the closet door for the third time, wavering between the impulse to invite herself to church, or remain in her room until Q and her son left. Standing before the mirror in a black bra and matching panties, she massaged baby oil evenly over her arms with enough vigor to spark a fire.

She'd wanted nothing to do with their God yesterday? But that was before she understood the power He could give her. Lord knew she needed it.

Tammie let her hand glide down her slick sides and over her flat tummy. She turned for a side view. Other than a few stretch marks beneath her belly button and accenting her hips, no one would know she'd had a child.

Q does. She wrapped her arms around her middle, recalling their laundry room intimacy. His God-assisted restraint fueled the beast inside, waking desire's sleeping volcano. All night, she'd tossed and wrestled sheets.

Ignoring him had failed. Working harder gave her a temporary high only to crash lower than where she'd begun once she reached home. Give her another week like this and she'd walk away from her five-year plan and beg Q to stick around.

Her body might not show her age, but her eyes told a different story. The whites had dimmed, ruptured blood vessels were visible, and the permanent droop kept things in prospective. She was too old to repeat the same mistakes of her youth.

Give in to your desire, you fail. Deny them, and you succeed. Sick of her reflection, she opened the closet a fourth time.

A quick grab and pull exposed her meager wardrobe. Fluttering tags hung from garments her sister so lovingly provided. She rubbed the tingle at the corner of her eyes. One day she'd get the chance to show Tee how much she appreciated all her sister had done for her.

Tammie donned the red dress, removed the tag, and stepped into a pair of black pumps before she could change her mind. It hugged her curves and showcased sculpted calves. Half-way across the room, she grimaced. "I can't do it." Tammie flung herself across the bed. There had to be another way to get the power Q had.

"God, you don't play fair." She groaned and flipped on her back to aim her accusations into the palm-shaped fan blades. "My daddy kicked me out." Tears finally escaped from the corners of her eyes.

James Morris, her daddy, had joined the church and nothing they had was good enough from then on. Momma had to dress a certain way. No more parties. Tammie sniffed and ran a hand under her nose. He wouldn't even take her to the father-daughter dance like he'd done with Tee.

"Why is it all or nothing with You?" Tammie curled on her side into a tight ball experiencing the loss afresh.

When Daddy wasn't at work, he was at that church. If she wanted to get a few minutes of his time, she'd have to attend the long boring meetings. But she chose to stay home with Momma while Tee went with Daddy. Is that why he turned his back on her? It wasn't like he wanted her there, or he would have insisted she attend.

"Daddy, Q was there for me." A wail tore from her throat, and she buried her face in the mattress. "And I got pregnant. I'm not a bad person." She sobbed, too overwhelmed to fight the wave of emotions.

Dad had gotten what he wanted. Worked his way up the ranks. Her pregnancy came in the wake of her father being crowned assistant pastor. Rather than having to explain a pregnant daughter to his church family, he kicked her out.

"I'll get my independence without your help." She jabbed her finger skyward toward God. "Forgiving what my father did to me is impossible. You ask too much." Tammie stiffened rising to a sitting position.

She'd just have to try harder. Nikki, her ex-roommate at the shelter, had been badgering her to openly participate in group, thinking the group may give her the extra push she needed. This week she'd do it. She'd done pretty good on her own. She'd move into her apartment with Junior soon, too.

Changed into an orange t-shirt and leggings, Tammie went to join her family in the kitchen. "Morning, Tee." She sauntered to the stove where her sister flipped pancakes and tickled Tee's side.

"Stop girl, 'fore you make me burn breakfast." Tee squirmed out of the way of Tammie's next attack. "Get you a cup of coffee."

Balancing her mug, Tammie sat at the table facing the stove. Her first sip sent the hot liquid, laced with caffeine and sweet Irish Cream coffee creamer. Straight to the center of her core. It spread throughout her body gently nudging her senses to attention. "Mmmm."

"Mom!" Quan, Jr.'s eyes bulged, as he hopped into the room, surely shocked to see her sitting at the table on a Sunday morning.

Setting her coffee down, he hugged her. Her chair scraped the tiles as she tugged the boy into her lap and blubbered loud smooches on his neck. His laughter brightened the room. Loving him would always be the right decision.

Q tapped Junior on the shoulder. "Boy, you getting too heavy to crowd your mom's lap like that."

She'd missed his entrance, playing with their son. Bald head shining, suited to impress, and smelling better than the men's cologne counter in Dillard's, he helped Quan, Jr. hop to his feet. Leaving their son wedged securely between them, Q leaned in close and placed a soft kiss on her cheek. "Good morning."

The surge coursing through her body far exceeded the stimulation she'd ever received from her morning java ritual. But why had Q changed? The day before, he'd run from her. A crease crawled across his brow like a crack in a piece of glass. Her confusion must've shown. She'd never been good at concealing her feelings from him.

"Tee, did you know I love your sister." Q ran a hand over Tammie's shoulder. "This woman helped me realize something very important." He selected the chair across from hers, and Quan, Jr. showcasing all the teeth God blessed him with, sat next to him.

"I've been known to put two and three together and get five but what did she help you realize?" A belly laugh filled the room. Tee placed a platter of sausage, bacon, and potatoes in the center of the table then stacked the round cakes on another platter.

"Morning, everybody." Deac burned a path to his wife with Devon in his arms, and smothered Tee with kisses. She giggled as if he didn't greet her the same way every morning.

Tee swatted her husband on the butt as he hustled past her to buckle Devon into his high chair and take his place at the head of the table. "Sit down, man." She mildly scolded him. "Q is trying to tell us what Tammie taught him."

Tammie wrapped her hands around her heated cup to keep from drumming her nails against the table. Q wouldn't relay what happened in the laundry room, would he? Her knuckles began to match the off-white ceramic.

Q stood and received the food tray from Tee and added it to the spread. "God is a keeper. I've spent too much energy trying to keep myself saved. If I had the power to do that, I wouldn't need Him."

"Amen! You better preach, brother." Deac clapped and Devon imitated his father.

Syrup dispenser in hand, Tee sat next to her husband.

Q turned to face Tee. "Yesterday, Tammie enlightened me about a conversation the two of you shared." He sat and scooted in toward his empty plate.

"Really?" Tee's eyes widened to the size of the saucer beneath her coffee cup.

Tammie dropped her gaze. Should she make an excuse to leave? No. If he wanted to go there, she'd let him. But he better tell it like it happened.

He'd wanted her as much as she did him, she was sure of it. She'd felt his heart had raced with hers; felt the heat of his short breaths rushing down her neck.

"I've got a lot to learn about God. He's not a bunch of rules and regulations. I'm gonna mess up. I know I'm weak when it comes to Tammie. But yesterday God kept me from breaking my commitment to him. Ain't that right?" Q shared a look with her brother-in-law.

Oh-no. Deac knew what had happened between them. Why was Q doing this? Tammie longed for some sand to pitch her head beneath.

Q's chest inflated the longer he spoke. "I've got nothing to be ashamed of."

Tammie played with the hem of her shirt.

"I love my family, and I'm going to fight to earn your trust." Q shifted his gaze to Tammie. Sincerity poured from the toasted depths of his eyes daring her to doubt his words. "I plan to marry you and honor you with my name. I'm trusting God to save you. I'm just here to water you with love. I'll wait as long as it takes."

Quan, Jr. looked up at his daddy in a trance as if blind with adoration. Tee glowed. And Deac beamed with pride for his disciple-in-training prodigy. Was she the only one confused by his declaration?

She'd tried to seduce Q—her body tingled with the thought now—and he acted as if she'd imparted some great Biblical wisdom. By the way Deac eyed them a few minutes ago, he had an idea just how far she'd been willing to go.

"Let's eat up. Looks like these two need to talk." Tee passed the meat to her husband.

Tammie sipped her cooled brew out of routine, too numb to be bothered to eat. A cacophony of smacking lips, forks scrapes, and slurps streamed from her family while her own plate remained untouched.

Deac was the first to push his chair out. "I got to get ready. Don't want to be late for church."

Q extended a hand to his mentor. "Hey, don't wait up for us. Junior and I will stay home with Tammie today."

She gripped the table. "Don't make your God mad on my behalf. I'll be here when y'all get home."

Q shielded their son's ears with his massive hands. "Deac, Tam was all over me yesterday and now she's trying to run a brother off. I don't think she knows what she wants." He winked at the same time he uncovered Junior's ears. "Go get your play clothes on. We'll have devotion here as a family and share our playtime in the backyard with your mom."

Quan, Jr. skipped out the kitchen sporting a big grin. Tammy fidgeted in her seat not sure what she should be doing. "I didn't ask you to do this."

"Missing a Sunday isn't a crime. I don't go there to keep God from being angry with me. I go to fellowship with family. Today, I choose to be with you and Junior. God's not limited to a building. Wherever I am, He's with me. Will you sit with us as I go over the Sunday school lesson with Junior?"

"Since you're missing church and all, it's the least I can do." She forced herself to look at him. His magnetic smile pulled at her heartstrings, lifting the corners of her mouth like a master puppeteer.

Tee unbuckled Devin and swept him up into a hug as she exited the room in preparation of church.

Q jumped up. "Gotta change."

Soft as a gentle mist on a warm spring day, silence crept into the room. Did they teach something different at his church than they had at Daddy's? *Junior and I will stay at home with Tammie.* Q's words kindled an excitement for something more. What if there was more to Q's God than she'd learned in the past?

Tammie scrambled out of her stupor to clear the breakfast buffet. Q may want to use the table for their lesson. An overpowering giddiness snuck past her lips and she giggled.

Placing dishes in the sink, she envisioned Q and their son spending the day with her. She pictured the way she'd played house when she was a little girl—the husband, wife, and child living in the pink and white plastic mansion with a matching car outside. Oh yeah, and the dog. How could she forget Skipper?

The same way she'd forgotten dreams weren't real.

CHAPTER SEVEN

Parked in front of the KLTV 7 Building, Q ran a hand over the protective sheen he'd layered into his vinyl dash. Hot to the touch, it hinted at another scorching summer. Detailing the car should've wiped away Tam's scent, but it was worse than cigarette smoke, sticking to every fiber in his mind. Blasting the air-conditioning didn't help.

Tammie must've gotten stuck on a call. He turned off the engine and rolled down the windows. The skinny girl with glasses, too big for her head, walked out of the building. Q leaned forward. A few more familiar faces exited, but no Tammie.

He settled back in his seat. The leaves on the trees decorating the downtown corner blocks rustled in the wind. Heated drafts of thick air washed over his face, reminding him of the box fan in the bedroom of his grandma's house.

He had to have been close to seven, no older than Junior's eight years. Stripped down to his shorts, he'd listened to his voice warble through the plastic, rotating blades. His grandma, old and stooped, had warned him to stop before his spit shorted out her fan. Q chuckled. Spending more time with her than his negligent parents, he'd learned to entertain himself. Junior wouldn't have to live like that.

Had Tammie decided to ride the bus?

Q scanned the corner. A lone man stood waiting. The wind churned and lifted the hat off the fellow's head reminding him of Junior's pleas to fly his kite. Although it was a week night, a extra hour or two of play shouldn't keep him from getting his homework done. Maybe Tammie would join them and make it a family event.

She'd been so agreeable the past couple weeks. He'd like to say it was because she'd started going to church with them. But the questions she asked during the rides to work had come from places in the Bible not covered in the church service. She must've liked the new Study Bible he'd gifted her. A gentle ache spread through his chest.

If he'd known staying home with Tammie one Sunday would motivate church attendance, he'd have done it sooner. He'd prayed she'd find her answers like he had. Then what?

Strangers emerged from the KLTV 7 Building. He drummed his fingers on the dash. Waiting had never been his strength. But patience promised too many benefits he couldn't afford to miss. He didn't have to feed the meter since it was after five. Q reclined his seat and rested his eyelids.

Tammie opened the passenger door. "Why you sitting out here, sleeping in this heat? Turn on some air." She buckled herself in.

Q ran a hand over his mouth—nothing wet or crusty. The dash showed 5:45. "I was examining the inside of my eye—." His tongue stuck to the roof of his mouth. Up close, in this heat, the distortion to Tammie's face was obvious. Like a candle left burning too long, one side of her face drooped where the bone structure beneath had sustained damage. How had she endured so much at the hands of that monster? Compassion pooled into the back of his throat and he swallowed.

Tammie touched her eye and turned away.

"Don't." He covered her hand with his and pulled her toward him until she returned his gaze. "You're beautiful. I like your hair pulled back. Bangs are overrated."

Her big eyes shone with unshed tears. "You're not just saying that to make me feel better, are you?"

Since the day in the laundry room, he'd limited physical contact to a peck on the cheek or a hand to her lower back. But words would never reveal his heart. Q leaned close and brushed a tender kiss over the keloid scaring spattered in the corner of her eye. "I love everything about you." Salty tears splashed over his lips. He couldn't love this woman any more than he did right now. "I'm sorry I left you unprotected. If you give me another chance, I'll spend the rest of my days making it up to you."

Tammie pulled away and swipe her cheeks clean with the back of her hand. "What are you saying?"

He retrieved a napkin from his armrest and handed it to her. "I've said it from the beginning. I want you for my wife, but if you'll let me date you, take things slow, I'd like to start there." Q reached for Tam's hand.

She drew back and clutched her chest, shaking her head.

A knot formed in the pit of his stomach. Did she still love him, or had he misread things?

"So much has changed. I'm not who I used to be. Nor are you." Tammie grabbed his hand and squeezed when he straightened in his seat and looked ahead. "I'm trying to discover who I am right now. I can't do that in a relationship. I get lost."

The pleading in her voice shamed him. Q bowed his head. He was so busy getting her qualified to be his wife, he hadn't left room for her to get what she really needed from God, a relationship. Q tightened his grip on her hand, lifted his head, and looked her way. Love wasn't self-seeking. "If I made you uncomfortable, I apologize."

"We still good?" A tentative smile lifted the right side of her face.

"Friends. We have a son to raise."

She frowned. "Is that the only reason you want me around?"

Q palmed the back of his neck and blew hard. "Why you always making stuff more difficult than it is?" He stretched his fingers out over the steering wheel. "I'm his father if we're together, or not."

Tammie turned. "You've got a point."

A breeze swept through the car sending the Black Ice scented Little Trees car-freshener into a tailspin. He didn't control his future any more than he controlled the weather. *All I have is today. Tomorrow will take care of itself.* "Hey, it's a perfect day to fly kites. I plan to take

Junior to the park and catch some of this wind. You wanna join us?"

"Only if you'll take us to Andy's afterward for custard."

"When did you develop a sweet tooth?"

She clapped her hands and bounced in her seat. "You're looking at the new team lead representative. That's fifteen dollars an hour."

So, Tammie's new style wasn't for his benefit. Further proof, he'd been self-centered. The knot in his stomach convulsed. Q hoped the smile he'd meant to give hadn't come off as a grimace. "You did it. Explains the changes in your look."

What if God's plans for Tammie's life didn't include him?

Q cranked the car and boosted the sound on the radio before merging into the flow of traffic. Soon, he and the victory chants of Tye Tribett were moving down the road.

Hours later after picking up Junior and flying kites, Q walked over to Andy's newly renovated sitting area and handed Tammie her medium chocolate cone.

"Dad, what'd you get?" Junior bounced around in circles at Q's side, probably already feeling the effects of the root beer float he'd wolfed half-way down while they'd stood in line for the rest of their order.

Q grinned. "A pretzel caramel crunch concrete." Junior's exuberance was contagious. He laughed away his impulsive desire to mimic his son and jump up and down. Spending quality time with family had become the perfect antidote for his heavy heart.

"I want to taste it." Junior paused his circling long enough to perch his mouth open like a baby bird awaiting its meal.

Q spooned a chuck of vanilla ice cream, cluttered with caramel and pretzel chunks onto the boy's tongue.

"Me, too." Tammie closed her eyes and opened wide.

Would the torture ever end? Q sensed a check in his spirit. His flesh may have suffered a beating, but he'd grown closer to God because of the struggle, matured. *I count it joy.* He spooned a heaping spoonful into her gaping mouth.

She worked her mouth and swallowed. "I should've gotten that! It's to die for." Tammie quickly turned to slurp the brown cream running down her cone and onto her hand.

"Yeah, deadly." Q took his napkin and wiped the sweet treat painting the tip of her nose. "Let's get home."

Junior's got homework. And someone needs to get to work earlier so she can keep impressing upper management." Q hoped Tammie could see his sincerity. "I'm proud of you."

She beamed. "Thank you."

Walking to the car, Junior grabbed his arm. "But, Dad, I wanted to fly my kite some more."

"There will be another day."

"Yeah, but there's not always wind." Junior turned pleading eyes to his mother.

Q stopped in the middle of the walkway and held Junior's gaze, making another family go around. Although Tammie pushed a finger into Q's side urging him forward, he didn't budge. "What did I say?" Too often lately his son had a comeback for any directive he gave in the presence of Tammie. Good reason or not, best he put a stop to Junior's manipulation now.

Staring at the ground, Quan, Jr. released his arm and mumbled. "Another day."

Tammie stepped between them and bared her teeth. To another it might look like she smiled but he knew better. "It's still light outside. And the boy makes good grades. One day of extra play won't hurt."

"I said, no. So it stands." He'd explain himself to Tammie later, but he would not have his authority challenged in front of his son.

She snatched Junior's arm and flounced off toward the parking lot where the car was parked.

Q didn't change his stride. Tammie stood with her arms folded, waiting on him to unlock the doors. Better the boy learn now he couldn't have everything he wanted, when he wanted it. Delayed gratification built character.

Back at the house in the garage, Q let his family walk in without him. Better he cool down. The ride home might as well have been solitary confinement. He'd almost changed his mind and explained himself in the car ride to break the thick silence, but old teaching wouldn't let him.

Discipline was never discussed in front of children. If Tammie didn't agree with his decision to leave, it never should've been questioned in front of Junior. They had to be a unified front or kids manipulated things. At least that's what he'd heard his Pawpaw say often to his Grandma.

Before Tammie had come into the household, his son hadn't questioned his decisions. Maybe it had been the way he looked to his mother when Q told him another day. The calculation in the boy's eyes had riled him. Q would have a sit down with him, man to man.

Deac rapped his knuckle on the car's hood. "I hear congratulations are in order! When will you make the announcement?"

Q got out the car and checked the trunk. "Another day. Too much has already happened in this one."

Deac reached Q's side and held out a hand.

He grabbed hold and Deac reeled him in for a chest bump.

His mentor didn't release him when Q tried to step back. "Talk to me."

"Give me a minute." He moved to the side of the car and peered into the back seat. No kite. The place at his temples thumped. He walked over to the big toy bin lined against the garage wall. "I guess he took it in. But he knows the rules."

"Whatcha looking for?"

"Junior's kite. Outside toys don't go in the house."

"He's playing with it in the back yard. I heard him ask his momma."

One... Heat riddled his core. *Two*... Beads of sweat broke out over his head. *Three*... He swiped moisture dotting his upper lip. *Four*...

Deac approached Q. "Hey, man. Calm down. It's just a toy."

Q clenched his fists. "I told him, no. The path of a hard-head leads to destruction. Prisons are full of people who're willing to do anything to get what they want."

"But that's not going to happen to Junior. He has his father to lead and guide him. Take this opportunity to teach. Share your testimony with your son, the early decisions that got you there." Deac laid a hand on Q's shoulder. "You can't do it in anger. If Moses couldn't smite the rock, you don't get to handle His people any kind of way."

Q relaxed his fists and ran wet palms over his cargo shorts, dislodging Deac's hand. "They were a rebellious bunch."

"So are we." Deac spoke from a place of knowledge. All dirt had been aired at the group meetings.

Q grunted. "You right."

The door leading into the kitchen opened and Tee stuck her head out. "Dinner's ready."

"Thanks babe, we'll be right in." Deac waited until his wife closed the door. "Don't let your testimony be damaged. Remember, this is a time to celebrate. You earned an early release from parole. Things are going well and the devil mad.

"How'd you find out?" Q wiped a hand over his head.

"Your parole office sent the termination letter along with a notice for us to no longer forward status reports from the Father's Heart program. Just know, you can stay here as long as you want."

"Thanks, but I already found a place. Mr. Anderson introduced me to the elderly widow, Mable Cooper, at the church after morning meeting. He spoke up for me. She's not able to live on her own anymore. Moving in with her daughter." Q shuffled his feet. "She's willing to let me rent her own house with the option to buy if I make the first year's payments on time."

Deac raised a brow. "A house?"

"It's in the older neighborhood, but you know I can hold mine down."

Deac scrunched his brow and frowned.

"Don't worry. I plan on protecting my family the right way, winning the respect of the neighborhood. My gang banging days are over." He pounded his chest once, "Time I give back to those I took so much from. Lot of boys hanging on those streets needing a mentor."

"You make my heart swell with pride." Deac hugged him.

Q allowed the praise to mend some of the old places neglected by his own father. When he stepped back, he couldn't help but lift his head a little higher.

Deac pat him on the back. "Let's go eat."

"You go on. I'm not hungry." Q crawled back into the driver's seat and leaned his head against the steering wheel. "Forgive me, Lord. I can't count the times I've defied You. How dare I be angry with my son when you showered me with love and patience? Teach me how to love him. To instruct him in the ways he should go."

Calmed, he left the garage. There had to be consequences for Junior's actions, but which one to choose weighed Q's shoulders down. Then, there was the talk he'd have with his son's mother. This father stuff was so much more than he'd ever understood.

Had his dad struggled to do the right things? True compassion for the man he'd called father touched him for the first time.

Q wandered into the back yard. The hairs on the back of his neck lifted. He measured each breath and struggled to hold his peace, waiting on the Holy Spirit to instruct him. He folded his arms and rested on his heels.

Maybe five minutes passed before Junior noticed him and jumped. Staring wide-eyed at him, Junior's grip failed and the kite ripped from his hands with the next gust of wind. Q rushed forward and grabbed hold of the wooden spool before it could get away.

"I'm sorry, Dad." Junior eyed the ground so diligently, he could've been speaking to the ants.

Q turned away from his son and reeled the kite in. "Nope, you're feeling guilt from getting caught. If I hadn't been standing here, you'd still be flying that kite. If you were sorry for your actions, you would've come in and confessed your wrong doing." He held the toy out to his son. This had to be Junior's decision. "Here. Play until your heart's content."

He took it, but never broke eye contact with Q. Junior's chin quivered as if he might shed a tear.

Proud of the way his son had held his gaze, mind obviously working, Q lifted his chin and started walking toward the house. *Help him Lord, like you did me. I trust You.* Each step brought an assurance his son would do the right thing.

"Daddy?" Junior ran up to his side. "You mad at me?"

Q stopped and faced Junior. "No. Disappointed that you'd disobey me. I thought you understood I only wanted what was best for you. If you feel like you need to lie and manipulate me and your mother to get your way, then I've failed."

Junior thrust the kite in Q's hand. "Take it. I don't want it anymore. I'd rather play with you."

"You don't know how good that makes your old man feel, but not today, son. You need time to consider what you did wrong. There's consequences to our actions. Just like you, I did the very things my grandma and pawpaw told me not to do. Did you know lying got me five years in prison?"

"No, sir." Junior buried his head in Q's side and whimpered between sobs. "I'm sorry Daddy. I just couldn't help myself. But it wasn't worth it. I had more fun when we did it together."

Q stroked Junior's back until he went quiet at his side. "I understand temptation. The Bible teaches us to pluck out anything that offends us or more plainly get rid of anything that keeps us from doing the right things. You may need to put the kite in a place you can't get to it when you're tempted to disobey."

"I guess that's the same as Tyrone hiding Auntie's debit card at the first of the month. She has a bad habit of buying drugs. Another strike and they'll lock her up."

A queasiness washed over Q's stomach. How much time had Junior spent with his delinquent cousin while he was away?

Q gripped the boy's shoulder. "Something like that."

"Just get rid of it. I'm too tempted."

"You sure."

"Yes, sir. I don't want to wind-up like Auntie."

Q gripped the kite and brought it down over his knee. The wooden frame splintered and he finished ripping it into halves. "Son, God is able to keep you. We'll find a way for you to earn a new kite when the time is right.

***

Tammie lifted a glass and peered out the kitchen window. Her heart stuttered and she dropped the dish into the sink and ran out the house.

CHAPTER EIGHT

Tammie stormed the backyard and thrust her pointer finger against Q's chest. "How dare you!"

He tilted his head and turned on a blank stare as if she'd spoken a foreign language.

Forget him. She knelt down, eye level with Quan, Jr. and pat-inspected his squirming body. "Are you okay?" When she tried to pull the waistband of his athletic shorts, he pushed out of her arms. "Where did he hit you?"

"Mom!" Junior held out both hands as if to ward off any additional searches. "What are you talking about?"

"Never mind." Tammie stood and glared at Q. If he wasn't so tall, she'd have lined her nose up with his. "Go in the house, Quan. I'll take care of this."

"But Mom—"

"Go!" Tammie didn't dare turn to watch him run off, but waited to hear the door slam before she started shouting at Q. "Don't you ever step foot near my son again.

You pack yo stuff and get out my sister's house before I call the cops."

Q stepped back. He tucked the broken kite halves into a back pocket. Something, anything to keep them out of sight. His ramrod carriage exuded a confidence, inciting her fury all the more.

"You think I won't?" Tammie spun on her heels.

Q hooked her beneath both arms, lifted her slightly, and carried her over to the covered patio area.

She stiffened. "Take your hands off me."

"I don't doubt your promises. But I do question your reasoning." Q's soft words deescalated her tirade.

Like a tea kettle rattling on the stovetop as it boiled water, her body shook.

"What makes you believe I'd raise a hand to our son?" Q hugged her tighter, then stroked the side of her face.

"I saw you out the kitchen window." Tammie cringed, irritated by the pathetic whine in her voice.

"Did you see me strike Junior?"

Tammie twisted her body to the left, but failed to break free of his embrace.

He loosened his hold but didn't let go. "Let's talk things out. I don't know what you think you saw, but I promise I didn't hit him."

"I'm not asking. Let. Me. Go."

Q released her, but didn't step back.

Tammie spun around and scowled. "I won't apologize. I might've missed the signs before, but not this time. Never again will my son suffer at the hands of a man because of me." She looked beyond the tears pooling in Q's eyes. "I don't care if you donated the seed."

"Are you telling me Fred hit my boy?"

Tammie wrapped her arms around herself and rocked. "I came home from work. The house was trashed. Lamps broken. Coffee table littered with drug paraphernalia." She stumbled backward and sat hard in the cushioned lawn chair. "He'd never laid a hand on me before. I asked for Quan, Jr.'s whereabouts and the blows started. I don't remember anything after the second punch to the face. All I know is my baby come to visit me in the hospital busted up almost as much as me. CPS was asking questions I couldn't answer. If it wasn't for Tee and Deac intervening, I don't know where we'd be today." Tammie gripped the iron arm rests. Pain shot through her fingers. "I learned later he'd been hitting him for some time. All weekend long, I'd work and leave my baby in his care. My boy never said a word. He called himself protecting me." She cradled her head in her hands and let her long-held agony spill through her fingers.

Q lifted Tammie to her feet and hugged her tight. "Oh baby, don't cry. I should've been there. You didn't know." He stroked her arm. "Call Junior. He'll tell you. I didn't hit 'im. We agreed to destroy the toy. We worked out a plan to earn another one. I promise, that's all that happened."

Tammie backed out of his arms. "But... the way you acted at Andy's. I could see the anger pulsing big in the vein going down the side of your neck. You scared me. I've been a nervous wreck since we got home." She wrung her hands. "All this is just too much for me. You. Me. Living in the same house. It's making me crazy."

Q cleared his throat.

She looked into eyes so flat they could've belonged to a dead man.

"You'll be happy to know, I'm moving out. You see, I got off parole early." The corners of his mouth twisted half-mast. "I'm sure I can make arrangements to be out of here by this weekend." With every word, he backed away. "Things'll be better for you then. I'll make sure to send money for you and Junior."

She knew she needed to say something, but what? Everything had happened so fast. Q turned and walked into the house. At the click of the door, an intense spasm rippled across her chest. Was telling him to leave the right thing to do? Tammie pressed the palm of her hand against her breast bone. If so, then why did her heart hurt so badly?

***

Tammie trudged down the neighborhood block toward her sister's house. She wore the strain of the last two weeks on her shoulders like a hiker weighed down with his backpack. She entered the kitchen from the garage door.

"Where's Quan, Jr?" Tammie barely heard Tee's hello.

Her sister lifted the plate from the dishwasher rack and stored it in the adjacent cabinet. "He's in his room getting ready for bed." She stuck out a hand to keep Tammie from walking past her. "Take a seat at the table. Q should be pulling up any minute. Time we had a talk."

"It's only 6:30. I rushed home tonight to make sure I didn't miss tucking him in."

"He picked over his meal and went to his room immediately afterward. It's become his habit."

"Why didn't you tell me?"

"I tried. I keep telling you we need to talk but you're out of here so early in the morning—"

Two knocks interrupted the conversation.

Q stuck his head in the door. "Okay to come in?"

"Sure." Tee waved him in and gathered him close for a big hug.

As if her body recalled what it felt like to be snuggled up next to his, heat pooled into Tammie's belly and spread. Simple jeans and a t-shirt had never looked more enticing.

Quan, Jr. burst through the doorway. "Daddy, Daddy!"

Thank goodness, the attention was drawn to her son and away from her. She cooled her cheeks with her hands.

Q lifted the boy for a hug and nuzzled his neck. He had to be inhaling the little boy scent Quan, Jr. had denied her lately.

What she wouldn't do to have his thin arms wrapped around her. Since the day Q had packed his car and left, Quan, Jr. kept her at a distance. She rubbed the tingle at the corner of her eyes. Why hadn't he visited the boy? She'd warned him not to come back, but that wouldn't have stopped him before.

Her son's smile illuminated the room.

Tammie's breath caught in the splendor of it and she smiled. Her extra gifts and her attempts at video games on the weekends had won her a lame thank you, but no real joy like she witnessed now. Her pulse raced and she took a big soothing breath. She wasn't ready to admit there'd been a chasm in her own life since Q'd been gone.

She'd missed their early morning breakfast. The rides to work— not that she abhorred the bus, but there was never the same person to greet her or ask to hear about her day. A small part of her wanted to be adored. She yearned for Q's long glances. They made her feel attractive despite the permanent scarring from Fred's abuse. Then he'd touch her ever so politely—a hand to the back to guide her through the crowd, to pull her from the car, a tender caress to the cheek.

Tammie startled to catch herself staring at Q, his gaze locked on her. "I've got to go change." She choked out.

Tee put her hand on her hip. "Don't be long. Fifteen minutes. More than that and I'll climb those stairs. A good sister wouldn't make me haul all this extra—" She slapped her rump. "…around on this bad knee." Tee hobbled a few paces.

"Your knees are fine, and a little extra fluff never hurt nobody." Tammie looked away, refusing to be her sister's audience.

Tammie hurried to her room to change. Her lungs burned. Until she put some distance between herself and Q, she wouldn't be able to settle down and get the oxygen she needed.

***

Tammie waited until Tee left the room before she dared look in Q's direction. Across the kitchen table, he stared into space, appearing as uncomfortable as she felt. While she appreciated her sister letting her and Quan, Jr. live here, the meddling in her business... What?

She'd seen how the child had stowed away in his room the last two weeks. She talked to his teacher when the woman called concerned about the drastic drop in his homework scores. Her sister had done what she hadn't— took action.

Q stopped spinning the salt shaker on the table and looked at Tammie. "Tee's right. We have to think of Junior. He's been through so many changes. What can I do?"

"We can start back with the family activities you'd created." Tammie hated how her voice sounded puny.

What happened to the strong woman who'd refused this man's marriage proposal and cried independence? *Wimping out, that's what.*

He straightened in his seat. "Let me pick y'all up this Sunday for church."

Tammie wrung moist hands. She'd only worked up the nerve to attend Wednesday night services, not the big one that marked a person a believer. And she hadn't been in two weeks. Would people look at her strange?

"I'm not trying to pressure you, but Junior loves when we go as a family." He begged her with his beautiful dark chocolate, brown eyes.

Tammie toyed with the edge of the tablecloth. "There's no inching into the shallow end and working your way to the deep with you, is there?"

"You can pick a different activity."

"No, no. Church it is. But will you consider picking Junior up from school again on your days off?"

"Sure." He studied the wall behind her.

Tam reached across the table and covered his hand. "I need to apologize. I should've believed you when you said you never hit Junior. I had no right to tell you to stay away from your son."

"You were protecting him. Something I failed to do. You didn't keep me away from my son. I did. I couldn't face him. Or You."

Tammie bit her bottom lip to keep from going to him. If she could wipe the torture from his face, she would.

"Five years I spent in prison for a father who couldn't care less. Not once did I stop to consider how my actions would affect my own son. Figured he was too young for it to make a difference." He moved his hand from her warmth and ran it over his smooth head. "I don't deserve y'all."

Never had she seen him so broken. So low. "Don't say that. The boy idolizes you. Since you been out, you've made up for any time lost."

Hadn't her bad choices left Quan, Jr. unprotected? Understanding the low feelings that came with seeing herself as a failure, she had to go to Q.

Tammie stood behind him and wrapped her arms around his shoulders, squeezing tight. "My aftercare counselors teach us to accept the things we can't change. Your God forgives, right?"

Q nodded and put his hands around hers, clasped together over his pounding chest. "I just didn't know how to grab on to it. Didn't feel I deserved forgiveness."

"Well, that boy of yours sure gave it to you tonight. Now that you'll be hanging out with him again, he may send a little love my way. He never said it, but Tee told me he overheard our argument. He blames me for your moving out."

Q pulled her around and down to sit on his lap. "I'll talk to him." He circled her waist, and she turned in his arms for a hug.

Tammie sniffled. "He's been so sad. I'm hardly home to comfort him. Tee had to stand in for me and play momma."

He rubbed her back. "Let's go over your schedule, and I'll see where I can help more."

"That's just it. How will I ever learn to do things on my own if I keep needing you and Tee to help me make it?" Tammie pulled out of his arms and stood. "When I move out of here, it's just me and Quan, Jr. Y'all don't get it, do you? I won't feel complete inside until I succeed at something on my own."

There he goes with them pleading eyes again. Did he feel sorry for her?

"The void you feel can't be filled with achievements. We weren't made to be independent of God's presence in our life. I know." He thumbed his chest.

"In that prison, when I realized I could do nothing to earn my daddy's love, I finally did what the preacher said. I cried out to God to fix the ache on the inside." Voice thick, he paused. "And He did. A wholeness came into my life."

Head cocked to the side, she rolled her neck. "Then what was all this grieving I witnessed, if you so whole?"

"Self-inflicted punishment." He stood up, towering over her and enfolded her in his arms. "Thank God for mercy. He even used you to remind me I'm not perfect, but His love is."

Q had changed so much from the man she'd known back in the day. At least on the inside, that is. She snuggled against the warm body she remembered a little too well. Considering how he wasn't a part of her five-year career plans, she'd let herself enjoy this moment. She wasn't giving in to her desires per se, just taking a small sample to hold her until she could prove to be self-sufficient.

CHAPTER NINE

Q unlocked the house, walked back to the car, and opened the door for a blindfolded Tammie. She smelled of sweet vanilla wafers, making his mouth water. "Take my hand." Her slender fingers slipped into his, and he pulled her to her feet.

"What about me?" Junior called from the back seat, eyes covered.

"Hold on, son. You're next." He led her into the front yard, heart beating fast, excited to show her his new home. Hopefully, their future dwelling. "Don't peek while I go get Junior."

"I won't. But if you keep taking so long, I might. It's hot out here. Another second and the oil rubbed into the back of my neck'll be sizzling." Tammie smiled big.

"Does that part of the body even get ashy?"

"After treating the dry skin on my face, arms, and legs, might as well cover the entire body so it all shines the same."

Q paused to appreciate her loveliness.

Anyone else in a simple pair of skinny jeans, a pink striped blouse, and hair secured in a ponytail, wouldn't have gotten his attention these days, but this was Tam. He reveled in the beauty of her full lips and sassy attitude. He whiffed faint traces of the strawberry Blow Pop she'd just rewrapped and deposited in his cup holder. Mingled with her cookie fragrance, he craved a three-tiered strawberry shortcake.

"Are you still there?" Tammie turned and swiped the air.

"Going." He jumped out of her reach and ran back to the car to get Junior.

When both Tammie and Junior stood in front of the house waiting, Q removed his son's blindfold.

"Wow, Daddy, this ours?"

"Not fair! Remove this right now, or I'm going to rip it off." Tammie yanked at the bandana and Q quickly helped her loosen the knot.

"You're so impatient." Unable to resist, he trailed the back of his hand down the satiny skin of her neck before he clasped her shoulder. "What do you think?"

"Oh, Q. For this neighborhood, barred windows and all, it's almost middle class living." She turned and one arm hugged him before running ahead. Walking the porch, she tipped the paired rockers into motion.

Junior hopped on the wooden swing. "Momma, this nice, ain't it?"

"Yeah baby, it is." Tammie looked up at Q. "Your Daddy did good."

He'd spend the rest of his days doing anything she asked to keep her eyes shining with pleasure. Q leaned against the support post closest to the porch stairs and entry door. "You gone come look inside?"

"I like how it's got a fenced front yard. What about the back?" Tammie walked toward him.

"Yeah, Mrs. Cooper's children were concerned with reports of increased gang activity and burglary in the area. There's the chain linked and privacy fencing in the back to hide the graffiti. They had all that installed when they barred the windows." He motioned her forward with a hand to the dip in her lower back, as they entered the house. "After you."

"My room? Daddy you said I'd have my own room." Junior ran past them and headed down the hall.

"Last room on the left." Q chuckled, wrapped an arm around Tammie's waist and tugged. "Wait for it." He whispered so close to her ear his bottom lip brushed against the bubbled lobe.

"Yay!" Junior ran out into the hallway. "When, Dad? Where did you get it?" Junior didn't wait for an answer, but rushed back inside the room.

Tammie turned in Q's arms. "What has him so excited?"

Q dropped a quick kiss on her nose before grabbing her hand and pulling her down the hall and into their son's bedroom. "Welcome to the WWE!" His impersonation of the wrestling announcer sounded pretty good in his own ears.

She gasped and placed a hand over her heart. "Oh my!"

Junior traced the lower half of the life-sized Fat Head poster he could reach. "John Cena, Momma. It's John Cena. Don't he look real?"

"Yeah, baby. This is far better than any apartment complex." Her words drug out like stringed gum being pulled along from the bottom of someone's shoe.

While Junior marveled over the WWE bedding, locker, and rug combo, Q bent close to Tammie's face, but she avoided looking at him. What had gone wrong? "Son, play in here for a while. I need to speak to your mother."

She crossed her arms.

Q gently nudged her rigid body. This wasn't a competition on who could provide the most for Junior. Maybe he needed to remind her he wanted her to live here, too. As his *wife*.

She planted her feet.

"Really? Is this your way of getting me to pick you up and carry you around?" He smiled.

She sighed and walked out of the room back into the hallway.

He shut Junior's door and pointed to the closed one on the opposite end. "Don't be jealous. I ordered some things for our room. But you can't see that until we're married." When she didn't laugh at his play on humor, he lifted her chin.

She looked away.

"What's wrong? One minute you happy and the next this." He shrugged. "I don't get it. What did I do to make you mad this time?"

"I'm not mad." She turned and ran a hand along the textured wall. "This is an old house, but the updates are lovely."

He reached out and touched her shoulder. "Sad, then?"

She flipped around, back flush with the wall. "The fake wood floors make it look rich, but it's warm and homey. Junior's gon' love it here."

"I hope so. What about you?" Q tucked an escaped strand of hair behind her ear. "You haven't seen nothing 'til you see the kitchen."

Tammie covered his hand and pressed her cheek into his palm. "You're a good father."

While her words stroked his ego, warning bells sounded in the recesses of his mind. What *wasn't* she saying? "Thank you. And you're a wonderful mother."

He closed the distance between them intending to search her eyes for the answers. Why he feathered his lips across her mouth, he couldn't explain, but when she wrapped her arms around his neck and kissed him back, he pulled her in tight as if to make them one.

Tammie pressed a hand to his cheek and smacked a tiny kiss across his lips one last time before letting him go. "Who could be mad at you? What if it takes me years to get settled and be ready for marriage? I don't expect you to wait around for me. If anything, you've made me think about something much more important."

"I'm not in a hurry. I'll wait." He nuzzled her neck, not ready for the connection to end. "Think about what?"

She pressed a finger over his mouth. "Shhhh. Not today. Show me the back yard. I'm sure you and Quan, Jr. will spend a lot of time there."

"Okay, let's finish the tour." Q put his arm around her shoulder and pulled Tammie close to his side. Didn't she know he'd gotten the house for all of them? Then why did she keep repeating references to him and Junior, excluding herself from the equation? If not today, tomorrow. She needed to talk. He didn't want her clamming up on him again.

***

"Thanks for the ride." Tammie faced Tee after she exited the family van, in front of *For My Sisters*, the aftercare facility for battered women.

"Not so fast." Her sister held a piece of paper out the driver's side window. "In case you haven't memorized it, here's my number if I'm not back before you finish. Is this the group session or will you see the private counselor after the morning meeting?"

"Just group. Take your time getting your errands done. I don't mind having to wait for you."

"Make sure you open up. You been walking around looking like Pig-pen the last couple days. Instead of a dust cloud, melancholy been billowing around you all black and gloomy."

"Yes, mother. I'll try my best." Tammie scrunched up both sides of her mouth and waved again. This time her sister left the circled drive.

Entering the surprisingly warm and inviting, metal building trimmed in brick, Tammie lifted the clipboard from the ledge stationed at the check-in window ledge and signed her name.

The receptionist slid the glass panel to the right and pulled Tammie's white label from the sheet. "Thank you, Miss Morris. You can come on back at the buzz."

Conversations bounced off the walls in the medium-sized meeting room. She didn't cover her ears, but the noise levels warranted the childish reaction. She scanned the group for Nikki.

Her old shelter roomie had always looked out for her. She'd save her a seat. Many nights, she'd cried on her friend's shoulder. Nikki never let her stay down on herself too long. "*It's what you do with today that counts*," she'd say.

Tammie checked the clock on the wall. Two minutes 'til ten. She moseyed over to a chair and slumped down. Even if her friend came right now, they wouldn't get a chance to talk. She yanked the ponytail holder off and finger combed loose hairs to re-secure a better hold. The infamous, escape artists had curled against the side of her face resurrecting unwanted images of Q tucking the strand of hair behind her ear at his house.

Everything she'd ever wanted sat at the corner of Martin Luther King and Jones Road. A little white-frame house, with a porch, and the two men she loved most. Q had made it a home, and Junior needed that.

Could she let her son go?

Nikki where are you? Her friend had sent her kids to live with their biological father and his wife months ago. How did she know that was the best decision? Did her kids resent her? Or feel abandoned? A heaviness suppressed her next breath. She'd never want her child to suffer the insecurity and heartache that came with being forgotten.

But she'd visit. Tell Quan, Jr. how much she loved him. Go on any family outing Q planned, if she wasn't working. She sat up in her chair. He'd be mindful of her work schedule. Hadn't he proved to be Mr. Thoughtful? Or she wouldn't be considering sending Quan, Jr. to live with him.

"Sorry for the delay, ladies." Community Counseling Outreach Specialist, Amy Brown, rushed into the room followed by a petite black woman with soft curly hair framing her cute face. "We have a special guest for today's session. Please welcome Darlene Greene of the Ina Mae Greene Foundation."

The pretty lady stepped up to the mic. "Hello, everyone. Our slogan: Because the road to safety should never be a dead-end." The speaker may have been in her late fifties, maybe early sixties, but she was one of those women who appeared to transcend time, her youthful looks attractive. "Never tell your abuser you're leaving." Warmth exuded from her tender smile, while the slight cut of her bicep muscle made you believe she'd whop you a good one if she had to defend herself. "Do you have a safety plan? Seeing luggage or any signs that you're leaving him..."

Where was Nikki? Tammie swiveled around to the clock. 10:50.

"Better yet, just go. When your life is on the line, who cares about clothes? Can anyone share their escape plan?" The little lady pointed to the pregnant woman with her hand held high.

When had these others come? Advocates, counselors, and the chaplain stood along the walls, whispering softly among themselves. Tammie darted glances between staff members and the battered women occupying the metal fold-out chairs. Why was the crisis team here? A chill ran down her back, and she shivered.

What had the woman said? Because the road to safety should never be a dead-end. Tammie looked at the empty chair next to her. Where *was* Nikki?

CHAPTER TEN

Since the door stood ajar, Q rushed into Tammie's bedroom and sat beside her on the edge of the bed. "I came as soon as Tee told me about Nikki's death."

"Did you know the FBI says that a woman who tries to leave her abuser has a seventy-five percent chance of being murdered by him? Mrs. Greene told us at group today." Tammie wouldn't look at him. Did she speak to him or mumble into the air?

"Is she one of the counselors at the aftercare center?" He hoped a direct question would draw her gaze.

"A guest speaker for Ina something… A foundation named after her late sister. The abuser who took Ina's life discovered she'd packed her luggage." Tammie spoke into her lap as if the Hello Kitty printed pajama pants had inquired.

"You're supposed to be napping." He cupped her shoulders, gently nudging her to lie down against the pillow.

She shrugged out of his grasp. "I've rested enough."

Q covered her knuckles where she bunched the bedding in a death grip. "Passing out and resting are two different things."

"Tee talks too much." Tammie made the scolding sound like a weary afterthought.

Was this how grief looked on her? If tears flowed down Tammie's face or her voice trembled, he might know how to comfort her. Q pulled her limp body against him and cradled her head. "I'm sorry your friend died."

"Three times she'd tried to leave him." Her words vibrated across his chest.

Q rocked back and forth. "It's been an emotional day. You really should get some sleep. Junior likes to go to Sunday school, so I'll be here to pick y'all up early tomorrow."

Tammie shrank out of his embrace. "I can't. Why don't you have Quan, Jr. pack his things and spend the night? That way you won't have to make a trip over here to get him in the morning."

With the absence of her body pressed next to his, a chill settled in, matching the coolness of her tone. "I'll have him get enough clothes for the week." Q tested to see if he could get an authentic response from his usually feisty girl. He was desperate to spark some life back into her.

"Yeah, whatever you think is best." She wrung her hands in her lap and swayed back and forth.

"Tammie. Lay down. You're tired."

She slumped over and stared. At what?

Q sprang from the bed, stuck his head out the door, and shouted into the hallway. "Tee. Get up here, quick." He went back to Tammie and lifted her into his arms. Flinging pillows to the floor, he pulled back the comforter and placed her in the middle of the mattress. He tucked her in tight. "I'll have Junior home tomorrow after church."

She curled into a ball and faced the wall.

Q closed his eyes for a second. Inhaled. Blew it out. If only he could shoulder her pain.

"What's the matter?" Tee rushed into the room, huffing to catch her breath.

Q opened his eyes. "Look at her. She's not acting right. She would have let me take Junior for a week."

"She's probably still in shock." Tee got in the bed and wrapped her arm around her sister, gentle like she would Devon. "I know you're hurting. Right now, don't think on things you feel you should have done. Yesterday is gone. Focus on today. Tell Nikki you love her."

Q swallowed hard. *Lord God, Tammie needs You. Comfort her.*

"Why?" Tam whispered. "Whyyyy?" Her voice cracked and unleashed a strange wail. She turned into her sister's arms and sobbed.

Tee rocked her like a baby, cooing in her ear. "That's right, let it out."

"If only I'd called. Maybe she wouldn't have gone back to him." She cried harder. "I got too busy. Work. Family outings. Bible study. I should have been there for her."

"It's not your fault. Nikki wouldn't want you blaming yourself like this." Tee rubbed her back.

Q tiptoed out, gathered Junior's things, and they headed home. While God used Tee to execute the physical comfort, he'd focus on the spiritual. Tammie needed both.

He took the right into his driveway. How he arrived home without incident, most of the trip there forgotten while he'd render all praises to God. "Junior, Daddy needs some time to himself. I need you to play in your room for a spell. Can you I trust you to do that?"

"Yes, sir." His son straightened, adding another inch to his growing body.

He palmed his head and pulled him in for a quick hug. "You make me proud. I don't deserve a son like you, but I'm glad God saw fit to bless me." Q stepped back. "Now run along, and don't go outside. I'll lock us in."

"Love you too, Dad." Junior darted down the hall and toward his room.

As soon as Q crossed through the threshold of the master suite, he knelt, dropped his head to the mattress, and prayed.

I will comfort them and turn their mourning into joy, their sorrow into gladness.

Q clambered to his feet. Where had he heard the message before? From the top of his dresser, he grabbed the leather-bound journal he carried to church. He combed through his most recent entries. Not in sermon notes. Maybe in his scribblings? Notes marked morning devotion? There. Two weeks past, he found the scripture he searched for. Thirteenth verse in Jeremiah 31. Israel's Return Home. He read it from the page this time. "I will comfort them and turn their mourning into joy, their sorrow into gladness. Jeremiah 31:13)

Peace washed over him, removing the grime of worry that had lingered with him since finding Tam so lost in grief. "It's all a part of your plan, isn't it?" He gripped the book with one hand and pressed it against the beat of his heart. "Forgive my anxiety. Watching her suffer is torture. I love her so much, I got distracted from the truth."

He rambled through his nightstand to snag a pen and sat on the bed with his journal. Q studied his notes. Three knocks filled his room. Had he lost track of time?

"Dad, can I get something to eat out the kitchen? I'm hungry."

Q jumped up and opened the door. He'd have to get used to Junior being in the house. "Sure, son. You never have to ask to eat. Let me show you where everything is." He led Junior into the kitchen. "Just don't try to handle the stove. There's plenty of microwave stuff in the pantry. But why don't I put on a pizza for now?"

"Yes!" Junior hopped around. Then he sat at the table while Q got dinner in the oven. "Is Mom going to be okay?" Junior must have picked up on his worries.

Q started to give the boy a generic answer when thoughts from that morning's scripture study cautioned him to be slow to speak. God restored Israel, but they were torn down to be built back up. The gladness came after the sadness. What would Tam have to endure first to gain her joy?

***

Monday morning, Tammie walked out of the call center manager's office. She counted the grooves in the carpet, berating herself all the way to her cubicle.

With a finger held up in the air, directing Tammie to wait, Nadine wheeled her chair out from her desk into the aisle as far as her headphone cord allowed without disconnecting from the computer. "Ma'am, let me put you on hold for just a moment." She pressed the headset's control button. "Don't you dare sign back in your computer without telling me what happened."

"I'm signing out for the day." Tammie input the codes to bring her phone out of the call cue and shut down her computer.

"They fired you?" Nadine attempted a raspy whisper but heads began popping up from surrounding work stations as if it were Groundhog Day.

"Suspended, for now. They'll contact me after a review. I got to go." Tammie didn't care who heard.

She spoke in the same even tone she'd used earlier in the office when she agreed to sign the written confession that she'd intentionally hung up the phone on the rude caller. Two sleepless nights didn't leave her with the tolerance it took to endure verbal abuse from anybody. Not even an upset customer.

"Did you tell them about your friend's death?"

Tammie frowned, regretting she'd told her cubicle neighbor anything—even if she was the sweetest gal she'd met since Nikki. "I messed up." She gulped air and hiked her chin to staunch the wave of emotions. "It's the story of my life."

"It's not over, until God says it's over. They need to know your emotional state." Nadine punched her hold button again. "Thanks for your patience. One more minute please." She advised the caller.

Like Tee and Q, Nadine professed God to be the answer to everything. From the first day of Tammie's employment, she'd been kind and always offered her help. Another mother figure.

Tammie snagged the older woman's hand. "No. Pray if you must, but please leave things alone." She pulled the clutched hand to her chest and turned what she hoped were pleading eyes on her friend. "Go back to your call. I'll talk to you later." She hooked her purse strap over her shoulder and left the KLTV 7 Building as the boss instructed.

Out of habit, her gaze instantly sought out Q's favorite corner parking space. It had been weeks since he'd given her a ride, but she yearned for the security of knowing he waited. Not one time had he missed being there, or been late the days he picked her up. Always waiting.

She dragged reluctant feet to the bus stop. Empty, of course. Those with jobs were at *their* job, unlike her. Tammie's next breath caught. If she arrived home now, Tee would know something was wrong and bombard her with questions. She'd kill time at The Foundry, the coffee shop Q and Junior frequented before picking her up from work.

Time seemed to stall. She'd finished her coffee hours ago, but wouldn't waste another penny. Especially with the uncertainty of having a steady income. As soon as the clock posted fifteen minutes before five, she booked out the door and down the sidewalk to catch the bus. Last to board, she dropped into the first seat and window-watched until they pulled into the neighborhood stop.

Exiting with her routine evening commuters, Tammie headed home. She rounded the corner only to slow her steps to assess the tall white man walking up her sister's drive. Dressed in a pressed button up, slacks, and loafers, the man made her suspect it was a business call, but it could be one of their church members.

They had one of those diverse memberships. A modern-day Noah's Ark if she had to describe it. Anybody could look around and find someone who looked like them. Tee had explained traditions and cultures didn't matter when everybody was reading and living the same Word. *One body,* she'd call it.

Thinking what her big sister would do, she forced a smile and greeted the man. "Can I help you?"

"Are you Tammie Morris?"

She felt her smile slip but didn't try to put it back in place. "That's me, why?"

He reached behind his back and pulled out a yellow envelope, folded, but not creased down the middle.

Tammie struggled to form the words. "What is this?"

The man had already turned and walked back to his car parked at the curb as he spoke over his shoulder. "Legal documents. You'll find case and lawyer information inside."

Numb fingers fumbled the clasp several times before she successfully retrieved the stack of papers. Tammie gasped. Fingers trembling, the documents littered the grass.

"The State of Texas vs. Fred Jeffers"

Tammie crumbled to the ground. "Oh, God. Have mercy. I can't face him in court."

CHAPTER ELEVEN

Tammie attempted to relax in the breakroom sipping her coffee. Between tentative slurps, she rotated the steaming cup and swirled the brown liquid.

"I'm glad to see you answering the phones again." Nadine claimed the chair next to Tammie. "We've been lost without our team lead. How are you?"

She settled her cup onto the table. "Confused. Numb."

LaShawn strolled in.

Tammie snapped her mouth shut.

Her co-worker crossed the room and opened the fridge. "Hey, ladies. How y'all doing?"

"Good. And you?" Nadine answered for the both of them.

"Can't complain." LaShawn grabbed a brown paper sack and tromped out of the room, allowing the door to swing closed. "Have a nice day."

Nadine leaned in and rubbed her shoulder. "Why aren't you eating? Do you need me to get you some lunch?"

"No. I'm not hungry." Tammie stared at her cup.

"You'll get your appetite back after the funeral. Just need some closure is all. Did they schedule the services seven days out to allow the one relative in California to fly in? Why can't we as a people get our dead buried? Everybody else manages to do it within three days or less."

Tammie laughed. She hadn't expected the short escape from the energy-sapping grief, but she did appreciated her friend's humor.

"Yeah, her aunt Alma. The service is this Saturday at eleven a.m. My sister had to step in and help. Nikki's family didn't have a home church. Tee booked them a chapel and a preacher at Christ Holiness Temple, at no charge." Tammie fingered random store circulars stacked at the end of the long table.

Nadine got up to pour herself a cup of coffee from the pot on the commercial burners next to the sink. "She's a part of Bishop Blackmoore's congregation, right?"

Tammie nodded. "He's not doing the service though. A visiting pastor, Nicholas Jones, is filling in."

Nadine skirted four chairs to set a glazed doughnut in front of Tammy. "They're complimentary for a reason."

Tammie turned up her nose.

"Don't make me use force." Nadine rested a hand on what should have been a hip. Being slight in stature, her loud, mouthy attitude was all the intimidation she could produce.

Nibbling the cold pastry must've satisfied, because the drill sergeant took her seat and blew into her cup.

"That's the good thing about mega churches." Nadine took a sip. "They have the additional resources to help others."

"Nikki's kids' daddy had to help with the funeral arrangements."

"Makes you wonder why they ever split up."

"So much can happen. My son's father went to prison for five years." Tammie flipped a couple pages of the Brookshire's circular, then pushed the stack of advertisements out of reach. "That's a long time to be away, raising a kid on your own. You hook up with someone who looks promising, not knowing you're too tired and emotionally drained to pick right." Tammie covered her face with both hands and shook side to side.

Nadine caressed her arm. "We all make mistakes. God must have something great planned for you. You survived and have the support of your family, then He spared your job."

Tammie uncovered her face. "And an apartment." She turned to Nadine. "I don't understand God. Saturday, I learned my friend died. Monday, I got suspended. Tuesday, Tee informed me my apartment is ready. Wednesday, I met with the committee and got my job back. Then there's the new Q, saved and Holy Ghost filled. Does God have to take in order to give?"

"Tell me if I'm wrong. Q is your son's father who used to pick you up in the burgundy Monte Carlo."

"Yes." Heat swept her cheeks.

"I assume the five-year prison sentence is the take away. 'Cause a saved version of the man you once knew has to be a gift. Are you saying y'all together now?"

Tammie grabbed her cup and swirled the coffee dregs. "We're not a couple."

"Then you want to be?"

"Yes. No." Tammie exhaled an exasperated sigh. "We're getting along and doing things together for Quan, Jr.'s sake."

"When did your feelings for him come back?"

Tammie straightened her back. "I can't afford to become dependent on nobody. You'd think I'd learned my lesson. I get served to appear in court and face my abuser, and you want to know what my first thought was?"

Nadine tipped her head to the left. "What?"

"Would Q come and support me? It's pathetic." Tammie drank from her cup and choked to get the cold mouthful down. She plopped the cup on the table and put her hands in her lap. "Daily he's arrived at the house with my boy to check on me after work, and I refuse to speak to him. At first, I thought sending Quan, Jr. home with him was all he wanted, but he keeps coming. Insisting I see him."

"He didn't know you'd been suspended?"

Tammie eyed the table. "No, I left the house at the same time every day."

"No wonder you're confused and numb. If I had to keep up with all those lies, I'd be crazy too." Nadine laughed.

"They shouldn't be bothered with my problems." Tammie didn't try to lower her voice.

"It's your family. We need one another." Nadine ran a calming hand over her shoulder. "Why do you think God created a match for Adam? Eve was the answer to his loneliness. His help. He paired us with man so we'd experience fellowship. Keep lying to yourself and pushing what seems like a good man away. You'll not only be numb but dead on the inside."

She pictured Q's big smile and broad shoulders, and grimaced when her body responded. "Depending on a man got me into the mess I'm in."

"Then don't. Put your trust in God. Marriage is honorable and fun, if I must say so myself." She flashed a saucy grin. "Don't be afraid to live. I bet you even breathe better when Q is around."

She wasn't about to validate Nadine's theory, but she couldn't keep from smiling. Her friend had a gift for painting things clearer. Could she really love Q and be free? She inhaled deeply. The thought seemed to purify the air. She'd never felt more like a prisoner than she had the past few days of her self-imposed separation from him.

Nadine pushed out from the table. "Think about what I told you. It's almost time for the twelve o'clock lunch crew to come. I need to visit the girl's room before I have to get back on the phones." She dropped her cup into the wastebasket, walked to the door, and turned a pointed stare toward Tammie. "Life is short. Don't put off for tomorrow what you can do today."

With Nadine gone, Tammie poured the rest of her cold coffee down the drain before trashing the cup. Maybe she'd ride the bus to Q's and surprise Quan, Jr. He needed to come home and start helping her pack. If his dad offered to help, she'd let him.

Instead of pushing Q away, she'd do what Nadine suggested. Live. At least a little.

After three steps toward the exit, her stomach grumbled and she doubled back to the refrigerator and found her lunch. She'd eat at her desk.

***

Aligning the same wall adorned with the gym's Christ Holiness Temple crest, Q scanned the weight rack. He gripped the 100 lb. dumbbells and plopped down on the bench. Leaning back, arms chest-width apart, he thrust upward.

"Hey man, you should've called me over to spot you." Catfish, Mr. Turner if they'd been in a group session, materialized above his head.

"I'm used to doing things on my own. In the pen, nobody has your back." Q pumped the irons, embracing the burn. "But I won't run you off," he spoke after he completed the first set of twelve.

"You've got the *look* again. What's her name?"

Q chuckled. "Obvious, huh?"

"Been there. Give me two more. Put your pent-up tension to use." Catfish coached.

"Her name's Tammie." Q tore into the next twelve reps. "Grrrr." He grunted out the extra two.

"That's what I'm talking about."

Q had never needed friends, but the comradery had its benefits. The continued flow of vocal challenges and encouragement from Catfish for the next hour successfully took his mind off Tammie.

Catfish followed him into the locker room after he racked the last of the weights they'd used. "You ready to talk about it?"

Q took the first lounger, and Catfish sat adjacent to him in the other, separated by a round table laden with bodybuilding magazines. "We were doing so good. Going on family outings the days I picked her up from work." His heart ached with the memory. "She even started attending Bible study with me and Junior. Then her friend died. She cut me off. Won't see me. Just Junior."

"What's your agenda?" He cocked a brow. "Marriage?"

Q sat forward in his chair. "You got something against commitment?"

"No." Wearing a smug grin, Catfish crossed his leg. "Just testing the depth of your feelings."

"There's no one else for me. Just her." Q moved to the edge of his seat.

Catfish squared his shoulders. "She saved?"

He dropped his gaze. The bottom row of blue lockers numbered ten across. "Not yet."

Catfish shook his head. "Take it from me. You don't want to move before God is finished working on that heart of hers."

"It's the reason I witness and invite her to come to church." He couldn't muster his earlier confidence, so his retort came out flat, if not dry.

"Seems like all there's left to do is surrender what you hold dear to God, Abraham."

"You got jokes." Q chuckled, but soon sobered at the earnest gleam in his friend's gaze.

"Nope, sacrifice never is. It's scary."

Didn't a true friend tell the truth, even if it hurt? He might not remember where, but the information had to be jotted in his study journal somewhere.

"Step back from the situation. Either you trust Him or you don't." Catfish stood. "Think about it."

Q jumped to his feet. Think? About the possibility of Tammie not being a part of God's plan for his life? He'd shower. Get Junior from school. Stop at the grocery store for dinner. Fill up his tank with gas. Anything to keep his mind too busy to *think*.

***

Tammie stood out front, locked outside of Q's front yard. Outside of their lives, Q's and Quan, Jr's.

If she lived here, she'd have dinner warming while she rocked on the front porch waiting for the menfolk to get home. Something about the thought settled in her stomach like a good meal after being really hungry.

She peeled her jacket from her damp arms and tied the sleeves around her waist. If she'd stopped to consider they might not be home when she arrived, she would've gone to Tee's first and changed from her work clothes.

Tammie walked an invisible line from one end of the fence to the other on tired feet. Waves lifting from the concrete discouraged her from going barefoot. Instead, she rubbed the sting from her bare arms where the intensity of the sun's rays beamed down. At the sound of a car pulling up, Tammie turned.

"Mom?" Quan, Jr. called from the passenger side of Q's shiny Monte Carlo.

Her breath hitched. She'd never been so glad to see the burgundy car. Or the smile on the face of the one driving. If she could trust her ability to read a man's eyes, Q's eyes—love, desire, and hope welcomed her presence. And for the first time all day, she breathed.

"Hello, baby boy. Q." She acknowledged him with a nod.

The car stopped at the curb, still running. Q rounded the front of the car and went to the lock at the gate. "I didn't know you were coming." He fumbled the key. "I'll have this opened in a jiffy. Junior crawl in the back and let your momma get under some air condition."

Tammie giggled and settled into the front seat.

Quan, Jr. scurried out and climbed in behind Tammie with his infectious smile in place.

Q bent to pick up the key and worked the padlock free.

She'd surprised him, but his obvious excitement to see her fulfilled a desire she hadn't experienced in a long time—to be wanted. Not the lustful urges from the past, but true companionship.

"You have a good day at school, baby boy?" She pulled her visor down and peered in the mirror to see him.

"Yes, ma'am." He bounced on his seat. "Momma, what you doing here?"

"I can't come to visit?"

"No. I mean… you probably can." Quan, Jr. squirmed, then turned eyes in search of rescue on his father as he got behind the wheel, put the car in gear, and drove into the yard. "Daddy, can't Momma come over here to see us?"

The tip of her ears burned. She inspected her nails, giving herself time to hide any embarrassment on her face before looking up and finding Q watching her.

He never turned to face their son but looked deep into her eyes. "Your mother is always welcome. I don't know what took her so long to come visit, but I'm glad she's here."

She looked away first. He'd asked her to marry him several times. She wanted to live, but it had to be on her terms. "My plan is to start coming more often."

"Why?" He covered her smaller hand, laying on the arm rest.

Tammie glanced at the mirror, again. Junior's gaze seemed to meet hers there, expecting what? "Does there have to be a reason?"

"You've been…" Q shut the engine off, removed the keys from the ignition, and passed them to Quan, Jr. "Go unlock the house. Then bring the keys back."

"Yes, sir." In the short time her son had been with his father, he'd dropped his habit of asking for an explanation. With him, anyway. Her boy jumped out of the car, unlocked the house, and brought Q the keys before he went inside without looking back or lingering.

She fidgeted with the knot of her jacket still tied around her waist while Q restarted the car and let the air flow. She'd have to have her jacket dry cleaned.

"Tammie." The huskiness in his voice ran through her veins, awakening delightful sensations throughout her body.

Why did she look up? Her gaze lingered on his lips before she caught herself and met his eye. By the smirk on his face, he'd witnessed her slip. Heat splashed her neck.

"You've refused to see me all week. Why are you all of the sudden, standing outside my house waiting?"

"I need Quan—"

He lifted a cautioning hand. "The look we shared on the other side of the gate had nothing to do with our son. Tell the truth. You need me as much as I need you." He dropped his hand and caressed her cheek.

She pressed his hand to the side of her face.

When he leaned in close, she remained still. Expecting his kiss.

Q leaned around and planted a whisper-soft caress to her cheek. Then the other.

She closed her eyes and breathed in his clean masculine musk. Any resistance to his charms over the past week vanished.

Hovering near her mouth, he whispered. "Admit it. You love me."

His nearness mesmerized. Why couldn't she reveal what was in her heart? Was it time to forget everything else and do what she did best? Love Q? Her chest ached to have his mouth possess hers. She leaned forward, hoping to coax him to finish what he'd started.

He pressed his lips to her eyelid. Then the other. "Look at me."

You'd think his kiss gave her the strength she'd lacked to hold her lashes open. She peered into his intense brown depths and cowered at the image reflected back at her. Tremors started in her stomach and spread over her body like a virus.

"Tammie? Tammie." Q stroked her face and cried in a weak voice. "What's wrong?"

CHAPTER TWELVE

Q pulled Tammie in as close as the car's armrest allowed and cradled her head against his pounding chest. Had he caused the raw fear in her eyes? "Baby, what just happened?"

After a minute, she pushed him and Q drew his arms from around her. "Now I know why predators like Fred seek me out. I saw it. In your eyes … Just now." Her voice wavered. "No matter what I do, it's still there. A weak little girl, needing a man to sustain her."

He reached out to comfort her, but she shook her head hard.

"I fought it. Gave it all I had. But, no matter. In the end, here I am. Then there's Quan, Jr. I've just about given him to you." A fat tear slipped down her cheek, probably opening the dam for others to flood the front of her shirt without making a sound. "And the crying. It's all I ever do. I'm sick of it. I'm sick of me."

The hair on the back of his neck rose. How many times had the Holy Spirit moved on him to allow room for her relationship with God to develop? Hadn't Catfish, not even two hours ago, advised him to release her into the Lord's hands? But, no. He'd rationalized his love for her. His need to protect her. Provide. More than God?

I've been a hindrance. Forgive me Lord. Today, I commit the very thing I desire most to you.

Q trapped his hands between his knees. "You're stronger than you think. Did a man help you win your job or answer the phones for you at work?" He leaned toward her, peering into her face, when she tried to avoid direct eye contact.

She picked at the fabric running along the edge of the seat. "No."

"Don't give man the credit God deserves. *He's* your help." Q rubbed his hands down the front of his joggers. "Give yourself time to heal. You've survived so much. I admire your strength."

Tammie swiped her face dry and straightened in her seat. "You're being kind."

"I'm being honest." He opened the glove box and handed her a napkin. "But I want you to get your big head out the car so I won't say anything else."

She laughed, brushing away a tear.

"For the record, you didn't turn your back on our son. You left him with me, his *father*, while you grieved." He closed the box and swapped the damp makeshift-tissues in her hand for dry ones. "You're a wonderful mother." Though small, a spark lit her dull eyes. "It takes a courageous woman to admit she fears love. God's softened your heart."

Although her mouth remained closed, she seemed to relax her shoulders.

Q reached behind the seat and deposited the soiled napkins in a plastic trash bag from the last oil change. "I'm sure you had a reason for showing up at my place? And the fact you stayed after finding us gone, it must be important."

"I came to get Quan, Jr. to help me move. If you'd happened to offer your assistance, I'd planned to accept the help." Red highlights blushed her cheeks, making her skin radiant.

His chest muscles tightened. She needed him. He gripped the steering wheel or he'd pull her back into his arms. "We've got to quit meeting up like this."

She dipped her head. "Like what?"

"Walking in a field littered with land mines." Hands off the wheel, he leaned over and kissed her scrunched forehead. He lifted her chin. "Remember the laundry room?" Thankfully, his finger had lingered on her jaw or he would've missed the vulnerability twinkling in her eyes before she looked away.

He spoke softly. "We share great passion. Left to ourselves, we're destined to make a move and detonate an explosion. But this time around, I want to celebrate us, like the finale at the upcoming Fourth of July festival." He stroked her cheek.

She looked up and held his gaze. "I'd like that."

"I know the funeral is Saturday. Go. Get some closure." Q lowered his hand to the armrest. "While you're there, let me take care of the moving. Junior and some of my buddies will do it in no time. Label the boxes where you want them to go." He turned in his seat. "After church Sunday, I'll bring Junior to you, so he can get ready for school. We can go over visitation." His grip found its way back to the steering wheel.

"You mad at me?" She pointed toward his hands.

"No." He squeezed, then released his tight hold on the wheel. "I'm doing what I should have done a long time ago. Listening." *Letting go.* He extended an open palm toward her.

Again, she tugged on the jacket knotted at her waist, then placed her hand in his.

"I'm going to give you time and space to do things on your own. Accomplish your goals." He kissed the downy skin across the back of her hand. "When you're ready, I'll be here. And bring the preacher." He grinned at the way her eyes bulged.

"You're crazy." Shaking her head, she slipped her hand free, smiling. "Don't you think that's being a little cocky?"

"That would mean I had confidence in myself." He took her fingers and brought them to his lips.

"If not yourself, then what?

Q kissed her knuckles. "Who. Ask me who."

She snatched her hand, crossed her arms, and glared at him.

He roared in laughter. "I'm waitin'."

"Who do you have confidence in? And don't tell me it's God." She rolled her neck and smacked her lips with an attitude.

"Then I won't." He turned the key and shut off the engine. "But it doesn't stop it from being true. Last one to the house has to cook dinner." Q scrambled from the car, dashed across the yard, and soared over the steps onto the porch. He glanced back.

Tammie promenaded soft curves toward him.

He groaned. "Did you hear me? This was a race."

She kept swaying those hips. Once she stepped onto the porch, Tammie darted for the door, put her hand on the knob, and turned. "I win!"

He winked. "I like cooking for my family."

"Whatever." Tammie spun around and sashayed into the house.

Q hung behind. "Lord, I've boasted in You. Show Yourself mighty. I need a wife. My wife."

***

Thunder rumbled overhead as rain pelted the church's roof. Tammie placed the last salt and pepper shaker in the center of the oblong table where the family would eat after the burial.

"Tammie." Tee pointed to the clock.

Eleven-fifteen loomed in red digital numbers.

Her sister slid a huge pan of rolls into the commercial oven while she instructed a team of ladies outfitted in purple t-shirts. Screen printed across the back, KITCHEN CREW spelled out in bold white letters. "You'll have to go without me. You've already missed walking in with the family." She rearranged a piece of bread that must've shifted on the tray.

"But I don't mind waiting for you." Tammie wrung her hands. She might as well get used to doing things alone.

"Sister Spencer, can you help me operate this oven? It's too fancy for me." A heavy-set lady with gray curls called over her shoulder while punching buttons on the panel above the silver door mounted on the wall.

Tee closed her oven door and moved toward the woman. "Go. I have too many new volunteers to leave them without leadership."

Tammie stared at Tee's back. "Okay." *Not really.*

She gripped the edge of the huge metal island laden with food prep. Thankfully, Tee hadn't seen her hesitation or she'd have likely dropped everything to accompany her.

Tammie shrugged out of the kitchen and into the hallway leading to the chapel where the funeral sounded as if it had already started. She hurried her steps.

Thick strains of an organ pulsed along the walls, sending chills up her arms. Standing at the entrance, a woman in a black skirt, red jacket, and white gloves, matching her blouse, handed Tammie a folded paper with a picture of Nikki on front. She swallowed the lump crowding her throat.

The gloved hand settled over her shoulder. "Are you okay? Will you need assistance being seated?"

Tammy rolled the flyer in her hand. "No, thank you. Is it crowded?"

A look, resembling pity, flashed over the nice attendant's face before she tucked it behind her professional mask. She'd seen the same expression so often since her injury, Tammie could spot it easily.

"Seating is plentiful, ma'am." She opened the door and waved her forward.

Too soon, the music slowed. Panic gripped her chest. She didn't want to bring any more attention to herself, being the only person standing in the middle of the aisle without the dark chords to drown out her steps. Tammie slid into the first empty row on the right. On the left, there were no bodies to hide behind.

The music faded out.

"We will now have the reading of the resolution." The young lady at the podium stepped back, and an older lady took her place.

Tammie scanned the room. Shades of black draped every person seated in the pews. The first three must've been reserved for family since they wore purple corsages identical to the ones pinned on Nikki's children. She'd favored that color.

The matron droned in a drab voice, "Be it resolved, that we bow in humble submission to Him who never makes a mistake..." Did she even know the family? Was this another member of Tee's church filling in?

Tammie opened her program to distance herself from the heaviness weighing on her chest. If she died today, would her funeral resemble this—empty pews and strangers? The storm's thunder reverberated through the room. She hugged her arms around herself.

"We'll now have the eulogy by Pastor Nicholas Jones."

Tammie glanced over her shoulder. Where was Tee?

The pastor stood, his white robe a bright light against the gloom in the chapel. "With permission from the family, I'm going to do things a little different." He tucked his Bible beneath his arm and walked down from the pulpit.

"Nicole Harris, who I will from this point on refer to as Nikki, had recently become my sister in Christ, accepting Jesus as Lord and Savior." He turned an expectant look on the crowd. "Aww, come on now, y'all too quiet in here for me."

Oh, Nikki. When? If you believed, why didn't you tell me? Regret stole her next breath. Hadn't Tammie attacked anyone who related her suffering to being a part of God's plan? Nikki had learned the hard way to avoid confrontation.

"We're supposed to get excited when another soul escapes hell's torment and gains the gift of eternal life in Heaven. This earthly life is filled with too much suffering to go to hell."

Pressure built behind Tammie's eyes.

"In the Gospels of Matthew, Mark, and John, three different accounts of Jesus walking on water are given. I recommend you read all three, but let's turn to Mark 6:52 after Jesus tells the troubled disciples, *'Be of good cheer! It is I; do not be afraid.'*"

Again, a cool draft fanned over her arms, and Tammie rubbed them.

"Paraphrasing verse fifty-two, we learn the disciples had hardened their hearts, therefore, they misunderstood the miracle of the loaves. How many of you have witnessed miracles and refused to give God credit?"

What miracles? God was just as absent as her father.

"Somebody in here can probably think back on their life and see how this could be their funeral. But, God." He preached.

Tammie gasped. How many times had Fred hit her? Which blow could have killed her? Killed Quan, Jr.?

She'd lived to see another day. A future with her son. And Q. Tammie shivered.

Miracles.

"You so hardened by those in your past who have offended you, you refuse to believe the good staring you in the eye balls."

Q's face from yesterday resurfaced. He'd sat at the head of the table after serving her and Quan, Jr. green beans, mac and cheese, and chicken strips. They'd been a family. Her chest ached. Maybe her heart was stone.

"Yes, the events that surrounded Nikki's death was tragic, but I petition you to learn what my sister here learned. It's never too late to call on the name of the Lord." He ran a hand over his head, full of curls. "Peter witnessed the miracle and tested to see if God was real. *'Lord, if it is You, command me to come to You on the water.'* When Peter came down out the boat, he walked on water."

Tammie couldn't sit still. Grabbing tissues from the box beside her, she wiped beneath her eyes and dumped them into her lap.

"Our sister Nikki, like Peter, asked God to bid her to come. Nikki surrendered the suffering of this life and exchanged it for the peace of God. You can have that today. Call on the name of the Lord, He saves. The altar is open."

Her heart pulsed in her chest, begging for the peace he described. Hadn't she tried it her way? *I have the job, a place to stay, everything I thought I wanted, but no peace.* Could she really have it by calling out to Him? Music trickled into her consciousness.

The pastor sang. "Jesus said here I stand, won't you please let me in…"

I'm so tired. I tried to fix my life, but I'm miserable. I want to live. Can I depend on You like Nadine boasted?

He extended a hand out to the crowd. "Won't you give your life today. Don't let this moment slip away."

"Nikki, were you trying to show me the way?" Tammie gripped the pew in front of her. *Lord, if it is You, bid me to come.*

The pastor locked gazes with her. "Don't harden your heart against all the good God has done. Unlike man,

God never fails. Come and be made whole. Let me pray with you."

When had she stood and walked out into the aisle, his petition slipping past her defenses?

She stumbled forward until she was standing in front of the preacher, tears streaming down her face.

The pastor leaned close to her ear. "God loves you. He desires to save you from your sin. Give you hope and peace. Is that what you want today?"

"Yes. I want to be free." Free to love.

"Whom the Son has set free is free indeed." He spoke with too much authority to doubt his words.

Joy, peace, and contentment flowed over years of frayed nerve-endings. "Oh, God, How could you love me? I've made so many mistakes." Just like my Daddy.

What if Quan, Jr. had treated her with the same scorn she'd shown her father? Her usual self-preservation reasoning failed to obstruct the remorse flowing through her heart in the midst of God's presence. *I'm sorry, Daddy. Forgive me for not saying goodbye. I did love you. I forgive you. We all mess up.*

"Nothing's impossible with God. If you're ready to receive His love, I'll pray and you repeat after me."

She shut her eyes and inhaled the sweet aroma of the oil he smeared across her forehead. Anticipation throbbed in her hands and she lifted them high. *Jesus, hear my cry. Save me from myself.*

The pastor prayed.

She repeated. "...I want to trust Him as my Savior and follow Him as Lord, from this day forward. Guide my life and help me to do your will."

"Welcome, into the body of Christ, my sister. Now go and tell somebody what God did for you today."

Tammie shook his hand. "I will, sir." She turned and rammed into something soft.

"You can start with me." Tee pulled Tammie into a tight hug. "Sorry it took me so long. But you'll never know how it made my heart leap to see you walk down that aisle. How does it feel to be a new creature? To be free?"

"Oh, Tee. Where shall I start? I want to laugh and cry. Run. Soar. Walk on water."

"Come with me to my office. Let's let this family finish what they came to do. I have information you'll need." Tee grabbed her hand and pulled her along like she would Devon. Tammie followed her sister, amazed to see others kneeling at the altar, and some standing in line for the Pastor to pray.

Who would've guessed she'd find her hope at a funeral?

CHAPTER THIRTEEN

"I know you full on the Holy Spirit, but your sister is starving and when you eating for two—"

"Ahhhh!" Tammie stood and leaned over the small round table to hug Tee. "How far along?"

Tee stepped back. "I go to the doctor, Monday. I've only done the home pregnancy test. But I know my body. The same things happened with Devon—tired all the time, can't stand the smell of bacon. And you know how much I love me some pig." Tee squealed. "I'm more excited about your rebirth."

A new creature, she'd called her. A clean slate. The euphoria to begin anew, without the weight of past mistakes forever mocking her, gave her an idea of what it would be like to ride in a hot air balloon. Tammie smiled so big the muscles in her face quivered. Jesus suffered that she might experience such joy?

She had to know more. As Tee suggested, she'd start in the four gospels. Maybe skip to John since it told of the life of Jesus. The urgency to get home and pore over the scriptures had her more jittery than the time she'd downed one espresso too many.

Warmth flooded her cheeks. "I wonder what Q will have to say?" Tammie bent over the table and gathered her study packet.

"Don't hide your face from me. I saw it. Love lit your eyes and you blushed." Tee plucked the folder from her hand and stroked Tammie's face. "What are you going to do about it?"

She burst out laughing. "Bring the preacher."

Tee scrunched her nose. "What?"

"The last time I spoke with Q, he told me to bring one."

"He ain't said nothing but a word. If I can get a funeral together in seven days for a complete stranger, you know I can whip up a wedding for my sister."

"Hold on. He wants to 'celebrate us like the finale at the Fourth of July.'"

"Is that what you want?"

"I want to live. Like the time we were at his house playing family."

"That's it then. Deac called while I was in the kitchen. Good thing this storm kept them cooped up at my house, unable to move your stuff. You'll stay with us."

"But—" Tammie's jaw hung open, giving flies the permission to land.

Tee lifted a hand and hurried to her desk calendar. "July's around the corner." She flipped May out of her way. "We have a little less than two weeks." She tapped a square with her acrylic fingernail. "I'll get the preacher out to the house today. You get Q to propose again. And we'll have us a Fourth of July wedding at y'all's place. What do you think?"

Tammie forced her mouth closed and her eyes dried from bulging open too long. "Let me catch my breath." She rubbed the grit from her eyes, waiting for the old fear to rise up and steal her joy. Like a momma rocking her baby, tranquility lulled any threat to her newly found peace.

How many times had Q repeated his desire to marry her? For them to be a family? "I think it's a wonderful idea. But, how?"

"Leave that to me. You go on home and finagle that proposal so you can finally say yes and take us all out of our misery." Tee slapped a hand over her chest and erupted into a deep belly laugh.

"I thought you were hungry?" Tammie struggled to hold a stern look.

"I am." She sighed. "I'll grab something out of the kitchen after I corner Pastor Jones and convince him to follow us home. Since I handle his calendar, I know the remainder of his day is clear. Too, he's a bachelor. His kind are always in need of a good, home-cooked meal. I can whip up some dinner and invite him over tonight." She moved to her desk, snagged her purse, and hauled it over her shoulder. "No need in you moving into the apartment. Someone on the waiting list needs it more than you. They'll understand. If not, we'll handle the details Monday."

Tammie pranced. "Don't you think we need to see what happens first?"

"Girl, please. The man's been waiting on you."

"And I thought Q was cocky."

"No, I'm your big sister. Big sisters know things. Trust me." She held out her arms.

Tammie rushed into them. "I love you."

"I know. Now go tell Q"

"Everybody I love might hear an announcement today. Tomorrow ain't promised."

***

Caught in the downpour walking home from the bus stop, Tammie kicked her shoes off in the laundry room. Mud caked the rubber soles from where she'd exited the chapel looking for the front entrance.

Which turn had led her into the church's construction site? Must've taken twenty minutes before she found her way out.

Tammie unfolded a green bath towel stacked on the folding table. She buried her nose into the fresh, warm lavender softness and shivered. A delightful giggle escaped her lips as she wrapped the downy cotton over her head, leaned forward, and gave her wet hair a brisk shimmy.

Tee and her organization. Boy, did she love that girl. But if she'd left her at the church rounding up the preacher, who was doing laundry?

"What did I tell you about us meeting like this?" Q's husky bass injected excitement throughout her senses.

Tammie thrust upright, catching the cloth with both hands as it slid from her head. She wrapped the towel around her soaked, clinging dress as she turned to face Q. Her mouth watered, his sweet musk reminding her of honey. "How long have you been standing there watching me?" She attempted a scolding, but her smile probably didn't make it convincing.

"I walked in just now. How long have you been home? I didn't hear the car." He gripped the empty basket in his hands as if she'd try to snatch it from him."

"You scared to be in this room with me?" She snorted.

"No." He pushed the basket into her hands, moved toward the island, and scooped the stacked towels as if he needed to keep a barrier between them.

Testing her theory, she stepped forward.

He darted to the washer, towels clutched to his chest.

A slow grin stretched across her face. "You're shaking in your—" She looked down. "Flip flops?" She could hear her mother's words, *No man wants a giggle box.* It didn't stop her from laughing.

"My shoes and socks were drenched. These are borrowed." He lifted his foot and inspected the beachwear as if he hadn't put them on.

Tammie struggled to breathe between outbursts. To think her stomach had been in knots. For what? This was Q. Changed, but for the better. "Don't be afraid." She exhaled. "Be of good cheer."

"Are you quoting the Bible?"

"The preacher from the service. He said that and a lot of other stuff. You don't have to be scared of me attacking you. I'm a new creature."

Q's arms dropped to his sides and the towels spilled onto the floor. His mouth moved but no sound came out. He eyed her for what seemed an hour, as if solving a complex math problem. "As in saved? You got saved at the funeral?"

The sides of his mouth twitched. His hands, like wings, lifted and flopped back down to his sides several times. He peered up at the ceiling and back to her. What was he thinking?

Tammie nodded. "I found peace." She took a step. "I forgave my daddy."

He cleared the towels and closed the gap between them. "Do you know what you're saying?" His eyes misted.

She smiled, familiar with the war going on behind his glistening gaze. Doubt. To finally have what you longed for in front of you, yet scared to reach out and embrace it for fear it didn't exist—that had been her walking down the chapel aisle. How long had the pastor offered peace before she took him at his word?

Tammie stroked his clenched jaw.

He dropped his head into her hand and nuzzled her palm, eyes closed.

"Haven't you been the one telling me I need a relationship with God? Amnesia again? Could it be the reception is bad and your brain don't work in here?"

Opening his eyes, he lifted his head and clasped her hand between his. "You got jokes?"

"No, I've got a preacher coming." She ran her foot over the fibers of the towels beneath her feet.

He knelt before her. "Who am I that God would give me the desires of my heart? Bless me? Tam, I really need you to spit it to me straight. No more talking in circles."

She ran a hand over his smooth bald head. Oh, the joy spilling past her lips, trilling around them like the birds announcing a new day. A new mercy. Her heart seemed to expand in her chest—with love for the only man she'd ever really wanted.

If she'd only waited for him and tried to understand his need to have his father's love. How would their lives have been different? She'd never have moved in with Fred. No, the past needed to remain in the past.

Tammie peered into his eyes. This time, the reflection in their depths didn't portray the helpless little girl she'd been, but the woman who'd survived hardship with the help of God. She cradled the sides of his face. "I've been set free. Now propose already."

He grinned. "Kiss me like you love me."

Learning a thing or two from the master himself, she restrained from raiding his delectable mouth and showered his face with rose petal kisses.

He wrapped his arms around her waist. "If you'll have me, I'll spend the rest of my days making up for the time we've lost."

"Yes. Yes. Yes. And no more mention of the past. All we have is today."

Q pulled her down into his arms and captured her lips.

Tammie held on tight. What they'd shared before paled in comparison to the celebration of two restored hearts.

"Pastor Jones, looks like we made it just in time."

Tammie scrambled out of Q's embrace.

Tee and the Pastor from the funeral filled the doorway wearing smiles.

Q stood. "She said, yes. Doesn't that call for a little extra affection?"

Tee wagged a finger. "Depends on whose measurements you using. So hold off on any more of that extra until we can get this Independence Day ceremony performed in two weeks." She giggled.

Q's wide-eyed gaze beamed down on Tammie. "It's really happening?"

Her inside melted. "Didn't you say you wanted a Fourth of July finale?" Tammie's voice caught.

He lifted her off the ground, pressing her into his chest.

Their hearts beat as one.

He buried his face in the curve of her neck and tears spilled hot against her skin. "Why, now?"

"Because I'm free to love you." She looped her arms around him and hugged him close.

"I love you so much."

Thank you, Lord. It may not be exactly what the preacher had meant, but she'd praise Him every day He saw fit to let her live.

EPILOGUE
1 Year Later

Tammie descended from the witness box, head held high. She crossed in front of the table where Fred Jeffers sat with his attorney.

In the time since she'd seen Fred, life hadn't been good to him. The corn rows crowning his receding hair line not only were out of place with the suit he wore, but they sported too much gray to give him the appearance of a hardened criminal. Only left him looking tired and old.

He sneered.

Her heart hurt for him. Did he know he was lost?

She paused and shook her head in his direction. His immaturity earned her pity.

Lord, who knows the root of his bitterness. We've all sinned and fallen short of Your glory. Bid him to come, and show him You are real.

Tammie smiled, then took her place on the courtroom bench next to Q.

He whispered, "You did great," then reached into to her lap and secured her hand in his. "Are you okay?"

"I am."

"And what about her?" He ran a hand over Tammie's extended belly.

"She'll be better once we leave here and get some chili." She laid her hand over his.

"And a sour pickle for dessert?"

Tammie grinned big. "Yep, you know me better than I know myself. Now sit back and stop talking."

He tugged her ear and sat tall in his seat, taking her hand with him.

***

Tammie slowly walked out of the courtroom next to her husband, his protective arm draped over her shoulder. The sun gently warmed the air, not too hot, or cold. The aroma of Mexican food from Rick's On the Square permeated the air downtown. "Guilty. I'm glad that's over."

Q kneaded the muscle in her shoulder. "Will you come back for the sentencing?"

"No." Resolve punctuated her words. "The last chapter of my past is closed as far as I'm concerned. No looking back."

"Do you have any regrets?"

Did he really need to ask? She'd have to do a better job conveying her feelings.

They cleared the courthouse steps and stopped in front of the parking meters lining Broadway.

Tammie turned to face Q. "Before you dared to love me to Jesus, I was just as lost as Fred back there in the courtroom. Today I stand before you whole. Delivered. What's to regret?"

He enveloped her in his arms. "You've come off the job. We've got a baby at home. One on the way. What happened to you wanting your independence?"

"Some cry wolf, I cried independence. I desired you even when I said I didn't. Fear is a prison that no longer has me bound. *"Whom the Son sets free..."*

Q smiled. *"Is free indeed."*

Dear Reader,

I pray you loved *A Cry for Independence* as much as I enjoyed writing this novella. Lena Nelson Dooley and Stacy Simmons pushed me to create Quan Jr.'s story.

This novella is based on sub plot characters from book one of *The Wounded Lamb Series: **BLISS***. It's still being reviewed for publishing, so your feedback on this novella is greatly appreciated. However, if I receive enough feedback I could be convinced to self-publish again.

I'd love to hear from my readers. You can visit with me at https://www.facebook.com/AuthorJoyMassenburge.

Thank you for reading A Cry for Independence. Please consider telling your friends or posting a short review on Amazon or Good reads.

Final edits by: Cathy Rueter

Made in the USA
Columbia, SC
02 September 2022